I0545904

BETTER THE DEVILS YOU KNOW...

FOLIE À DEUX

RUBY MEDJO

Copyright © 2022
No part of this book may be reproduced in any form or by any electronic
or mechanical means, including information storage and retrieval systems,
without written permission from the author, except for the use of brief
quotations in a book review.
This book is a work of fiction. Any resemblance to persons living or dead is
purely coincidental.
Published by Ruby Medjo
Cover and Interior Formatting by Charly Jade @DesignsByCharlyy

ALSO BY
RUBY MEDJO/JUNIPER HALE

Tear Me Down: The Enslaved Saga Book One
Folie À Deux: Prequel to the Villainous Heroes Series
The Game: Book One in the Villainous Heroes Series
Psychopathy: A Villainous Heroes Novella
Until Dawn: A Short, Monstrous Novella
Amongst the Wolves: A Short, Monstrous Novella

*To my love, thank you for being my safe place to create
a world all our own.*

PLAYLIST

"Bad Habits" — Ed Sheeran
"Twisted Games" — Night Panda & Krigarè
"Heart Upon My Sleeve" — Avicii & Imagine Dragons
"Shivers" — Ed Sheeran
"The Good, the Bad and the Dirty" — Panic! At the Disco
"Sail" —AWOLNATION
"Thunder / Young Dumb & Broke (Medley)" — Imagine Dragons & Khalid
"Rewrite the Stars" — Zac Efron & Zendaya

CONTENT WARNING:

This book is a dark work of fiction. Heed trigger warnings before reading. 18+ only! In this book you will find: Breath play/choking, consensual non-consent, praise/degradation, DVP, extreme body mods, edge-play, mask play, spitting, worship, and mentions of past abuse/trauma.

"We're all mad here."
—Lewis Carroll

CHAPTER ONE

JAMESON STEFANOV

I glare at the thick envelope on my desk as though it is some living entity. Cheek resting along my pointer finger, elbow grinding into the unforgivable black marble, I simply stare. I know what is in that fucking file. But bringing myself to open it? Something my cold fucking heart cannot do.

I'll wait until Tristan gets home, for I cannot make a decision of this magnitude without his approval.

Our empire is in a carefully balanced position, but not fallen yet. We've cousins in New York who'd be willing to help since our father is gone, though the Volkov's interests are beginning to morph into something new, likely in thanks to Maksim. Gone are the ways of old. Drugs, weapons—they don't pay the same anymore.

Secrets are the knives to twist now. Secrets are the way to bring an empire to its knees. And with our father dead and buried, we are vulnerable to the families who'd use us as a rung on a ladder. Family is the only thing you can trust anymore, and we are fresh out of immediate family.

The door to my office slams open, a furious Tristan in the doorway like some avenging angel. He wears his emotions on his sleeves and paints the most beautiful scenes with his knives. I, on the other hand, crave control and the thrill of power above all else.

I often wonder when our mother was pregnant with us if she felt that duality; the calm, tempered power and the unbridled strength.

I stare into my twin's steely eyes, his face contorted into a sneer, black hair wet from the rainstorm. He doesn't bother to push it out of his line of sight as he stomps forward, boots squelching on the equally black marble floors. I'd be pissed about the mess he's tracking in, but I realize that is simply a tendril of leftover fear of what our father would have done to us if he'd seen such disrespect.

We both bear the scars of his form of child rearing, but most are covered by ink now.

Those who don't know us cannot tell us apart, save for our hair and the differing collage of images forever ingrained in our skin.

We have no resemblance of our mother to remember her by. We are our father's children—his only children. His heirs.

Tristan splays his inked fingers on my desk—mine, because he is too irrational and wild to sit at a desk and crunch numbers. Mine, because he enforces and I command.

His cobalt eyes flick to the envelope and back to meet mine as a rumble of thunder claps over the Cascade mountain range. The heat from the roaring fireplace does nothing to diminish the ice in his gaze.

"You rang?" he growls through clenched teeth. I must've interrupted something...*fun*, for him to be so surly. Judging by the fleck of blood on his cheek, I can only guess at who endured the brunt of his anger today. If the vodka on his breath is any indication, I'd put my bets on a lowly civilian this time.

I nod to the thick, taunting envelope.

"We have a...*problem*."

His eyes flare, pupils expanding wide in the span of time it takes me to say the damning words. A sick smirk curls on his lips. Twin telepathy is real—he knows already, and the savage hunter in him is salivating.

The line of work we were born into does not require ethics or morals. As such, neither of us seem to have them in our daily lives, either. The very same excitement I can see in his eyes, in the way his body hums with charged currents, is the very same excitement that I feel thrumming through my chest at the same time.

We played our cards the best we could, but time has run out.

"Shall I?" I ask. He gives a slight dip of his chin, which I know is the only indication I will receive as his assent. Reaching beneath my desk, the wide, bumpy handle of my favorite knife slips into my grip, and I free it, slicing through the top of the envelope. He upends it, spilling the contents onto my desk like a gutted deer. Our eyes search the documents briefly, but it seems we both know the answer before we have to speak it into existence.

After all this time, she's finally ours.

The winding drive into downtown Seattle is a fucking nuisance, especially with Tristan bouncing his knee and drumming his fingers the entire time. Where he's always been fidgety, I've always been still as stone, patient.

"How long has she been there?" he hisses, the sound of his words emitted through clenched teeth. He's on edge already—has been for two days. Two days for a man like my brother is a fucking eternity. Two days for me is the perfect, sweetest amount of torture. I'm not sure if I should be honest; the truth may set him off. He will find out either way, though.

"She's been there for three. We found out two days ago—"

"*Jesus fucking Christ*," he hisses in our mother tongue. It has been long since we've been home to Moscow. Our business is here, currently, and the tantalizing thought of going home is one we cannot indulge. His anger often makes his tongue slip into words that are more comfortable for us to speak.

I glance casually at him.

"Keep it together," I demand quietly. He tosses me a sideways smirk.

"You know I am no good at that." I snort in response as the GPS guides me to the shithole office. I should have expected nothing more or less of a place like this, run by the state. My hands tighten on the steering wheel, Tristan's own anger seeping into me. *Poor little thing*, a voice in my head mocks. I maneuver into a spot and kill the engine, my hand lashing out to grip the neckline of Tristan's grey sweater. Though it is the beginning of September, it's already cold here.

"I'm fucking serious. Keep it together. The last thing we need is social services breathing down our necks—"

He wrenches himself out of my grip, his strength always matching mine. I am met with his darkest glare.

"You think I don't already understand the situation? What this means for us?"

"I think you're being led around by your cock—"

He doesn't wait for my admonishments as he throws open my car door, exits, and slams it for good measure. My teeth grind as he shoves his hands in his jeans pockets and heads toward the glass double doors without me, a slight drizzle beginning. Rubbing my hands along my face, I rip the keys out of the ignition and follow, the hopelessness of this place leaching out and grabbing a hold of my soul.

ALICE WINTERS

The kind social worker hands me yet another tissue, my styrofoam cup of cider abandoned on her cluttered desk. I've crumbled the first few into dust already. The clouds, this place—everything around me feels dull and gray now. My life should just be starting out. I should be looking forward to homecoming, football games, prom, stressing over SATs and college applications.

None of that matters anymore—not when the last people in this world I love are dead.

It started with the wreck on Snoqualmie Pass last year, the one that claimed my mother and step-father when they were in their prime. In their will, my aunt would become my guardian. Only, they'd written their will ten years prior—when aunt Mary didn't have lung cancer. I should be thankful I made it through one whole year with her, however horrifyingly hard, before—

"Oh, hello, sirs…how may I—"

I do not even need to look up to know they're here—their presence is stifling, charged, an entity of its own. I feel my eyes water anew as I shrink further into the old bench, the plastic covered foam crackling as I do so. I cannot bring myself to look at them. Something akin to burning shame and unrelenting fear courses through me and leaves me clammy and weak.

"Where is she?" One of them says, his voice so deep, so rough and guttural and utterly authoritative. I chance a peek at my social worker; she's gaping like a fish, cheeks ruddy, matching her flaming, bottle-red hair.

"Excuse him. He's just…overprotective." The other voice is smoother but no less deep, no less husky. The tinge of their Russian accents sets my heart racing. I haven't seen them in a year. Mom always sent them Christmas cards, and Vasily could be heard yelling at them in Russian over the phone more often than not. My relationship with my step-brothers is almost non-existent.

But they are my last of kin.

And they terrify me.

Cautiously, I lift my eyes, flinching as their furious faces come into view. Many have trouble telling them apart, but for me, it's always been easy. Perhaps it is my utter fear of them that makes their faces unique in my brain. Tristan is wild, unreserved, always running his hand through his inky hair to keep it out of his eyes. He's sporting a new piercing—a silver hoop nose ring. Jameson is always quiet—an unnerving kind of quiet, his hair shorter, his eyes seeing *everything*.

We've only spent a handful of days together since our parents wed those ten years ago. Each time, they ignored me for the most part, but when their eyes would crawl over my skin, I could always see something in their gazes—a type of rage I could never fathom. They hate me. I took their father's time, his love, his affection. I know it in my bones that they hate me for it. Vasily had always wanted a daughter, he'd told me a few months before the crash. His wife at the time had died of complications of a rare disease before she could give him any more children. He was kind to me—the father I needed when mine had beat my mother within an inch of her life and walked out on us.

I'll never understand their hatred for me. It's not like I chose this life, wanted it. But I can be gracious enough to accept it, to lay low and stay out of their way until I graduate. I'll make sure they don't even know I exist—even though the prospect of living with them is doing uncontrollable things to my lower stomach, things that make my cheeks burn and my eyes water.

My case worker clears her throat.

"Have a seat, gentlemen, and we can go over paperwork and what to expect in the coming months."

Jameson is the first to move, seating himself next to me on the old bench without acknowledging me in any way. He's wearing jeans and a black hoodie—simple. Heat radiates off him and makes me shiver in the dingy office. I can feel his eyes on me for a moment before he turns to

7

Tristan.

"We already know how to keep a person alive," Tristan grits out. The woman gapes again, glancing at Jameson for help. He turns to his twin, one hand on his knee, elbow up, as though he's about to spring from the chair and throttle him. He spits words in Russian that make Tristan growl something back in the same tongue and sink into the spot on the opposite side of me. Being between the two men who haunt my nightmares and dark, awful fantasies sends a shiver through me, and I curl in on myself. *Bad, bad, bad.*

"H-how long has it been since you've seen one another?" she asks. I feel Tristan shrug, his knee bouncing. He wears jeans as well, only he tends to dress a little nicer. The scent of their colognes is sucked in through my ragged breathing, their smells somehow unique and similar at the same time. I'd been cold before they got here—I'm always cold—but now I'm stifled.

"A year. Since the funeral," Jameson answers smoothly. She nods, straightening out her paperwork.

"You'll be responsible for Alice until she graduates, regardless of when she turns eighteen. Those are the laws of the state, and I should hope you'd keep her in the same school for her senior year," she says. Tristan shifts but Jameson answers, always the calm, authoritative mouthpiece for his brother. My stomach sinks. I turn eighteen next month, but knowing I have no money and nowhere to go—and with the pressing urge to get my diploma so I can escape to college—I am well and truly stuck. The money in the will is untouchable until I turn twenty-five, or unless the executors of the estate and the powers of attorney—shockingly Tristan and Jameson—decide to dole it out early.

I know they won't be kind enough to do that for me.

"We plan to, yes."

I peek up at Jameson, surprised at this; Seattle Prep is an

expensive school, one Vasily paid for because he wanted me to get into a good college. It is surprising that they are extending that small kindness to me.

Jameson's squared jaw ticks. The side of his neck that I can see is covered in an intricate, geometric tattoo. The line work is beautiful, the shading dots. I wonder how badly it hurt to get that.

"And housing accommodations. I know being young—"

"We own a home jointly. Five bedrooms, three baths. She'll have all the room and board she needs."

"Oh...lovely," she says, beginning to sound enamored. I suppose it is easy to fall into the lure of their devastating looks. My friends at school passed around our one family photo at a slumber party once and gushed over how *sexy* they are.

I perk at this too, though. I've never seen their home—never knew they lived near Seattle. I guess they like to keep to themselves. I tune out as she goes over the tedious things she's already discussed with me; the home visits, the routine check-ins, their responsibility for any and all medical bills. Tristan stands as soon as he signs the paperwork, exiting without another word. My heart sinks further at his callousness.

Jameson sighs, though from where I am seated, I hear the tendrils of a growl. He signs his portion, shaking the woman's hand.

"I apologize. He's less cultured in American ways than myself."

"Oh, not at all, dear."

I want to snort, but I find my humor is pretty much gone—has been since my mom and step-dad died. For as scary as Tristan is, Jameson slightly tops that with his broodiness. I can feel his stare, and I jump up out of my seat, clutching my oversized cardigan tighter around my frame. Bending to grab my duffle bag of clothes and things from aunt Mary's house, I snatch my hand back as his long tattooed fingers reach it before me and heft it up. As we both stand, he locks eyes with me, no trace of warmth or even pity swirling in those steel-coated irises. Not that I would take his pity, even if offered up on a silver platter.

"This is all you have?" he says. I can tell he's lightened his tone for my benefit, but it does nothing to take the coldness out of it, especially as his eyes narrow and his brows slant in distaste. Eyes watering again, I pull my lip between my teeth and manage a nod.

"The rest of her things can be picked up at the storage unit on Fifth Street. They open Monday at nine," she says cheerily, probably more chipper now that I'm leaving. Jameson nods. I give my case worker one last glance and the best smile I can muster before I follow the tall form of my step-brother out, my fate nearly killing me then and there.

TRISTAN STEFANOV

The car ride home is becoming unbearably silent. I clench my fists so tight my knuckles pop and crackle, rivaling the beating rain on the windshield. Every breath is a fight not to turn around and catch another glimpse of her.

I fucking hate myself, no matter how little morals I have. In our culture, in our line of work, family is everything. So what happens when the last time you saw your step-sister, you got a raging fucking hard-on seeing how beautiful she'd turned out to be? What happens when—no matter fucking what—you can't get her out of your fucked up mind, despite how wrong it is? The only thing worse is Jameson.

Why?

Because he feels the exact fucking same. Shouldn't have surprised me when he'd seen me staring at her and he'd simply clapped his hand on my shoulder, squeezed, and said: "Me, too."

Watching her shudder with sorrow that day, knowing she'd lost her mother and someone she viewed as her father, it was enough to brand itself into my brain. Something difficult to do but not impossible. Jameson, on the other hand, is cold as fucking ice. I don't think he feels one ounce of pity for her, for the situation she's now in. He's just as selfish as me.

Good thing we like to share—but only with each other.

I'm just about to turn around, to mouth off something smart and see how she reacts, when Jameson speaks. Fucker. He knows me too well.

"There's going to be some rules, Alice," he says, voice gravelly and infused with his trademark authority. I roll my eyes to the ominous clouds.

She sniffles from the back seat. Grinding my teeth, I fight the immediate need to turn around, to touch her, to show her some semblance of comfort. Something Jameson sucks at unless he's fucked a girl senseless beforehand. The desire becomes worse when her angelic voice speaks.

"O-okay…"

I turn my gaze to my twin and narrow my eyes.

"Maybe you should enlighten me as well, *podonok*."

11

His eyes flit to mine and then to the rearview mirror. I can't be sure, but I am almost certain his gaze softens. Fuck, he has it bad. He's only looked at one woman like that before in his life.

I do my best to envision her face, to paint it in my mind so I can abstain from actually looking. Long, thick, golden blonde hair. The tiniest little mouth with the poutiest pink lips I've ever seen. A sloped, tiny nose, and those fuck-me doll eyes with shades of indigo and azure. With the smattering of freckles and rounded, pink cheeks, I'd commit every sin in the world to own her. And her body? Petite but strong, a volleyball player. She's got a fierce streak. My cock hardens at the thought of pushing her to garner a reaction that will prove just how feisty she can be.

"School every day, good grades, no parties, no lying, no snooping," he says. *Way to be obvious, dipshit,* I think. Of course she'll be curious enough to snoop now.

"No boys," I grit out. Jameson's glare is like fire across my face, but I ignore him.

"I…I just want to f-finish school and go to college," she says meekly from the back, her voice so small, so full of sorrow she cannot hide. I can't help it; I turn and glance at her, my eyes stuck on her porcelain face, her wide eyes glossed with unshed tears.

I know she's afraid of us; father told us to stay away because she'd cried to her mother about it when she was little. It had enraged us both for a long time, him giving up his sons so easily for another child. We thought her a spoiled fucking brat, a manipulator. But when we saw her at the funeral, everything had changed. And as I stare at her now? As she stares back and her bottom lip wobbles?

I see her for who she is; a young woman lost in a vast sea, scared, alone, barely clinging to her last tendrils of hope like a life preserver in a rough storm. I am about to speak when Jameson beats me to it.

"Good. Then we shouldn't have any issues."

I offer her a small smile, just a slight upturn of my lips, and you'd think I growled at her by how she reacts. Cheeks blossoming in pink, eyes widening even further, lips falling open. I almost groan from how badly the sight of her makes my cock ache and strain to be free, to be wrapped up by those pouty lips, to be plunging into her innocence.

I turn back around, adjusting myself as sneakily as I can. Jameson snorts, but I know as soon as night falls he'll probably leave to go fuck some random.

Eventually, we pull into the garage beneath our modern, angular home, the black metal siding and windows jutting out into the evergreens. If she's impressed, she makes no indication. We exit, myself grabbing her bag this time as Jameson leads her inside with me following. I cannot help but let my eyes wander over her pert little body; tight ass encased in leggings, oversized cream cardigan hiding her subtle curves, her thick blonde hair swishing over her bony shoulders. I would feel more guilty about lusting over her, but she's the age of consent. I'd checked and re-checked before we picked her up.

Not that I plan to pounce as soon as she's settled. It is more for my own edification; I feel a little less like a scumbag now.

Jameson flicks on some lights and hangs up his keys as we enter the sprawling kitchen, and I set her duffle on the island counter, moving to retrieve a beer to stave off some of my lust. Popping the top off with a hiss, I toss the cap onto the concrete counter and eye her over my beer as Jameson sighs and rubs his hands all over his face. Poor thing is shivering, hugging herself in the open space. Like a bunny surrounded by voracious wolves.

"Bedrooms are upstairs. Yours will be between ours. I'll

take you shopping tomorrow for whatever shit you need."

God, could he sound any more callous?

Alice just nods, shoulders tensing. I can tell she's trying not to cry. The urge to bash my knuckles against Jameson's jaw is almost worse than the urge to throw her on the bed and lick her cunt until dawn. As soon as I think that, I wonder if she's let anyone else try that on her. Is she a prude? Has she had any romantic relationship before? Just the thought is enough to make me down my beer in one go.

"What do you want for food?" I ask, leaning back against the cupboards and crossing my arms. Her eyes flit to me, some of the fear simmering as she twists her hands together. After some fumbling, she shrugs.

"I'm...I won't be picky."

So selfless. My eyes flit to Jameson, but now he's staring at her with an intensity reserved for our line of work. His possessiveness should alarm me, but I am the same; she is ours. We will care for her needs, whatever they may be, no matter how fearful she is of us. My twin and I have yet to discuss...other things. Namely, the dangers of the lives we live. Her proximity to us now shouldn't put her in danger, but there's always a slight possibility.

But I know we'd both be dead before we let anyone harm her.

Chapter Two

ALICE

I've been settling in for two weeks now. The intensity of the Stefanov twins is unrivaled, but they leave me alone for the most part. Jameson took me shopping, nothing more than a silent shadow as I picked out bedding, a desk, a new mattress, and some new clothes. Wearing a uniform at school means less haggle when it comes to everyday wear. I still feel guilty when I think of him paying for all of my things.

Jameson also takes me to school each day, and sometimes Tristan picks me up. My friends stare and gawk—not because of their multitude of fancy cars, but because of *them*. Their tattoos, their squared jaws, their broad shoulders and height—they are handsome. But they are wild, and I am constantly on edge, waiting for their niceness to end, waiting for them to seek their revenge for how their father treated me.

It is Saturday, the house eerily quiet and empty. Aside from taking me to and from school, they are often gone. I stumbled upon Tristan in their home gym one morning, too nervous to linger and give him a reason to hate me even more as I turned and dashed away before he could see me. The sight of him shirtless, sweat running down the rivulets of his abs, disappearing into the V that led into his waistband…it had stolen my breath in a forbidden way.

Peeking my head out of my room, I glance up and down the desolate hall as rain batters the windows. I don't have my own TV, and I'm not about to ask for one. With my homework for the weekend complete, I have nothing to do. My school's play for winter this year is an adaptation of *The Greatest Showman*, and I want to try out for a part—*any* part. It's been so long since I've sang. Senior year feels like a good time to do all the things I've been too scared to do.

Padding to the sunken living room, I curl up in the middle of the couch with a throw blanket and flick on the screen, surfing through all their streaming services with the intent to become more inspired by watching the movie. I feel guilty doing so without permission, but the thought of asking them is worse than the fear of a reprimand. Besides, I've been on my best behavior.

Instead of finding the movie, I get sidetracked with all the Disney classics, burrowing down and choosing *Alice in Wonderland*. It was my mom's favorite. I don't realize I've dozed off until a reverberating bang echoes through the empty house, making me jump with a yelp as voices carry

down the hall. Definitely my step-brothers, but definitely…
women's?

It's well past dark, a new movie playing. Shit. I am
choked with fear, unable to move as the lights flip on and
blind me.

"Oh woooow," a woman says, sounding very inebriated.
"Your house is so…*hiccup*…huge…"

Biting my lip, I peek over the back of the couch and
into the kitchen. There Jameson stands, clearly furious, a
blonde woman in stilettos teetering by his side. Behind him
is Tristan with a red head, his eyes also narrowed at me. I
quickly get the hint and hop up, rushing past them to the
hall and stairs when Jameson's fingers wrap around my arm
and dig in.

"You have a…*hiccup*…girlfriend?" The drunk one
hisses. I meet Jameson's livid eyes and wish I can just
shrink on the spot. Without looking away, he growls
something to Tristan in Russian. Though Vasily taught me
some, it's a difficult language and I never fully caught on.
Tristan answers with a deep chuckle, and before I know
what's transpired, Jameson is towing me away as I stumble
to keep up.

I think he's going to lock me in my room. Maybe—God
forbid—hit me to teach me a lesson. Vasily was kind—
never raised a hand to me or my mother—but the fear is still
there. I've seen men at their worst. I know what to expect.

But my heart sprints away from me as a whimper leaves
my lips. He's taking me to the back of the house, to an area
yet explored. I think it is his office.

"I'm going to give you a lesson, little *babochka*, and
then I'll allow Tristan his turn."

His words are ominous as he opens the door and pulls
me through, but I dig in my heels and begin to fight him
off as best I can. The door slams closed, and he whirls as I

let out a squeak of fright. He's got me trapped between his arms and the door, and I press into the cool wood, closing my eyes tight, squeezing out tears.

"S-sorry, I-I'm sorry," I whimper. It takes a moment to realize he's let me go. Through my pinched eyelids, I can still see the darkness of his shadow, but some tension oozes out of my body—only to be replaced as he traces his finger along my jaw and whispers something I cannot understand. He repeats it in English.

"Open your eyes, little butterfly."

Chest tight with the beginnings of a panic attack, I obey, staring straight at his neck. He's wearing a black henley shirt, two buttons at the collar popped open to showcase the intricate pattern of ink on his throat. With a gentleness unbecoming of his size and nature, he curls his finger and tucks it under my chin, raising my gaze to his.

In the lowlight of his office, his eyes are like a writhing sea, his brows slanted as he studies me. My heaving chest ratchets up another notch, and a pathetic little cry leaves my lips. His eyes shift—his pupils dilate.

"You're right to fear us, *babochka.* We are dangerous men."

I can only manage a small nod as my head becomes light. I knew this already. It's an instinctual kind of fear, a primal kind that warns me I am much too close to danger for comfort. I muster my courage, gearing up to apologize again and swear I'll never even leave my room, but then he shifts, releasing my chin.

With a yelp, I bring my forearms up to protect my face and cower, shaking so hard and gasping in breaths. But nothing happens. My biological father used to get physical with me, my mother often stepping in to protect me. The memories of that night bubble up, and a choked sob escapes my lips as my knees wobble.

When I chance a peek, Jameson is an arm's length away, fists clenched at his sides, his jaw undulating as he grinds his teeth. His eyes are the worst, though; so dark, so menacing—so livid.

"Did my father…" he says through clenched teeth before he pauses, clearing his throat, leaning toward me as my harsh breathing calms slightly. "Did my father ever hit you, *babochka*?"

I am startled and quick to shake my head, feeling how wide my eyes have gone. I want to yell *No*, to protect Vasily and his memory. He was kind to me, loving and doting. I miss him almost as much as I miss my own mother.

Jameson's eyes narrow.

"Did he ever hurt Anna?" he says, his voice a low growl rumbling like thunder over the distance between us. Every muscle in my body is tense and locked. He looks so frightening in this moment, the veins in his hands pulsing, his tattooed forearms visible because of his pushed up sleeves. He's steel and I am aluminum foil.

Muted, I shake my head quickly again. He seems soothed—placated—which calms me a fraction more.

"I-I'm sorry—"

"Stop apologizing," he growls. I jump, and so does my heart, sprinting away just as it's calmed.

I can only manage a slight nod, shaking hand wiping at my tear stained cheeks.

"You need to spend more time outside of your room," he says, his accent thickening as his voice lowers. "It is not healthy for your mind to stay hidden away because of us."

Swallowing hard, I manage a nod, though I have no intentions of showing my face around the house more. It will just make me more miserable, seeing them, having to continue to bury my deplorable feelings while also fighting my depression.

He stares at me, his gaze so penetrating, raking over every inch of my body as I stay curled by the door, his eyes pinning me to the spot like a trapped butterfly on a board. Normally, I'd look away, too nervous to meet such an intense gaze, but for some reason, his actions have me curious. He didn't hit me, instead backed away and gave me space, and in that space between us, a sort of melancholy seems to grow. His eyes—normally hard, angry—are not right now. Intense, yes. But not mean.

It is a look I cannot place, one I've never seen before. I feel...safe...for the first time since my mom and Vasily died. I used to cry when it was time for bed, thinking my father would come back in the middle of the night to finish what he started. It took a while, but my mother and I made it through. And when she met Vasily? I was terrified of him, too, until he proved he would never harm us. I miss that feeling, knowing I am home and that no one can get to me. He'd even made it a game when I was younger, both of us walking the house at night before bed to check all the locks before he tucked me in.

The way Jameson is staring at me now is the same but also different—another layer added that I cannot decipher at the moment. I know my intuition is correct, though; I feel safe. My breathing has calmed, the panic attack slinking away to fight another day.

"What do you see when you look at me?" he asks, voice low and guttural. I swallow hard, already knowing my answer but afraid to speak it into existence. Maybe it is the knowledge that he is Vasily's son that makes me feel safe. Maybe it is his gaze, how strong and keen he is. Maybe it is him as a whole; utterly powerful.

I part my lips to answer when a knock on the door has me jumping away. Jameson growls something as Tristan pushes his way in and closes it. Heart racing, I now have him at my back and Jameson at my front. I wring my hands together and chew my lip until it bleeds. They exchange a few words in Russian before Tristan moves forward.

Keeping my eyes down, I tense, heat coming off him in waves. He's wearing a ripped gray sweatshirt that seems a little too tight across his muscled chest and bulging biceps, his dark jeans hugging his thick thighs.

"Little *babochka* is afraid?" he says, a teasing note to his voice. I wonder what it is they are calling me. I hope it's not something derogatory. Jameson snaps something at him, but Tristan doesn't seem to care. I flinch when he reaches for me, inadvertently bumping into a wall of pure muscle—Jameson. His scent is what hits me first; spicy pine and notes of fire. And then so does his sweltering body heat. Before I can jump away and apologize for touching him, his arm snakes around my side snugly, pulling me tight to him. My cheek brushes against his upper abs as he spits more venom at his brother.

He's...*protecting* me. The startling realization makes my head spin, and I glance first up at Jameson, who's staring down his twin as his Adam's apple bobs, his nostrils flared and his jaw ticking. His long fingers curl around my hip bone possessively as he squeezes me with the force of his words. Tristan is quiet, and when I flick my eyes to him, I find he's already staring at me, his own jaw clenched, his eyes wide and much easier to read than Jameson's.

In those steely depths, he looks...lost. Saddened. I wriggle, wondering what they have been saying to each other to make them look at me this way. Jameson gives me a squeeze and releases me. Shivering in the absence of his warmth, Tristan reaches out again, much slower this time. His long, tattooed fingers trace my jaw, his gray eyes overflowing with something that makes me blush and squirm. It isn't a bad look, but it's intense, and it's new,

23

and it almost reminds me of when Vasily would look at my mom.

"Do you want to watch a movie with us?" he asks, lips quirking up. I am stunned at his offer. Didn't they have… uhhh…women to attend to? I'm not that naïve; I know what men want, and those girls looked way more than willing. My skin crawls at the thought of them doing that with me in the room next door—and then another emotion takes root that I immediately banish; jealousy.

These are my step-brothers, for God's sake! But…now, after the intensity of this moment, I don't want them to go back out there to those girls. I want them to spend time with me. I've been alone for so long. Is it wrong of me to not want to share them? Is it wrong to revel in the safety they make me feel? Something I've been craving for a year now?

"O-okay, yeah…" I say. Tristan's smile morphs into a full-fledged grin, showing off his perfect teeth. Jameson moves forward, and I feel every inch of his body as it hovers just millimeters away from mine.

"We get to choose though, dear Alice."

"And we have…particular tastes."

JAMESON

Tristan got rid of those fuck-dolls for us. The two weeks

24

that we've had Alice has been utter torture; she barely comes out of her room, barely makes a peep or a fuss. Every morning, I have to watch her flee my Escalade in that plaid schoolgirl skirt, mouth watering and cock aching. My control is slipping, and Tristan's is nearly gone. We'd even gotten into a heated argument over the possibility of her dating until we both realized we are on the same side.

We cannot share her with another. Even the thought that she may have already had a boyfriend—a selfish prick with no balls—sets me off. She deserves so much more than a fumbling idiot who wouldn't appreciate her the way we would.

But that leaves us with our consciences. She's of age, soon will be eighteen which will considerably lessen our already thin resolves. The worst of it, though, has been tonight.

I'd planned to be stern with her, tell her to grow up and stop hiding away. It had also been a way for Tristan to make those women leave, and it had worked—until she'd flinched and cowered away from me.

In our line of work, we see that. Often. Wives of scummy men with black eyes pitifully covered by makeup. Daughters sent off to marry into lowly families to smooth tensions. The occasional trafficked woman presented to a group of leering men at a club for free entertainment.

I recognize the haunted look in Alice's eyes. She's no real reason to fear us; we've never even hugged her. Something else has happened, something in her past before our father married her mother. I intend to unearth it, but I also intend to check my attitude more. Perhaps be a little less...domineering.

"We need beer and food," Tristan grumbles. I roll my eyes, grabbing my keys off the hook before I even make it to the living room. I see what he's doing, so I throw him a devious smirk.

"Come to the store with me, Alice. You can pick out snacks and dinner."

She pauses in the hallway as Tristan's knuckles pop with the force of him clenching his hand, and my smirk grows.

"Umm...o-okay, let me get my shoes," she says softly, disappearing to her room. Smug, I cross my arms and level Tristan with a satisfied grin.

"Fuck you," he hisses, though I can tell it is good-natured; a small grin tugs at his lips. I give a shrug as Alice comes back, pulling on her rain coat. Fuck me, she's stunning, even all bundled up against the rain like she is.

"Be back soon," I drawl, heading to the garage with our little butterfly following willingly. The drive to the store is quiet, the cab of my car warm as the rain outside pounds the windshield and blurs the lights of the city as I take the next exit off the freeway. The silence with Alice isn't unnerving; it is filled with calm, with peace. Her scent swirls around my car; wildflowers and bergamot tea. Delectable. I chance a peek at her. Her thick golden hair begs for me to run my fingers through it, her ruddy cheek warm as thoughts I'll never know race through her keen, beautiful mind.

I don't want her to be depressed, but I know that's not something I can entirely control. The best I can offer her is a trip to a therapist, but I know she'll shoot that down at the moment. Better to simply be kind to her—more gentle and understanding so she feels comfortable enough to leave her damn room.

With a sigh, I pull into the grocery store parking lot, and we hop out. My eyes scan the lot for any threats as per usual, but now I am acutely aware of the petite presence next to me. I draw closer as we walk, resisting the urge to press my fingers to her lower back—resisting the urge to touch her.

It isn't busy this time of night on a Saturday, but that also means the frat boys and addicts are out en force. I cannot wait to have my patience tested. I lead the way to the beer aisle, grabbing Tristan's amber ale, before we meander wordlessly to the frozen pizza and dessert section.

"Well, pick your poison," I say, trying to keep my voice gentle. Her eyes jump to me, her teeth worrying her lip. She seems more relaxed, at the very least. Slow, timid, a small smile etches itself onto her devastatingly beautiful face, like the clouds parting and the sun shining after a hurricane. It hits me square in the chest.

"What do you like?"

For a second, I almost choke and sputter at her question, until I remember we are discussing types of pizza. Clearing my throat, I shrug.

"Anything you like is anything we will like as well. We aren't picky."

The way my voice lowers, the way her cheeks flush and her eyes gloss—I almost wonder if she catches the double meaning to my words. I smirk at her barely-hidden reaction, wondering just how attracted she might be to us. I nod to the frosty glass door.

"Go on. And for dessert, Tristan will love you forever if you buy him anything cookie dough."

She opens the door and grabs a few boxes of thick crust pizza—thankfully realizing we Stefanov brothers need a substantial bit of food to tide us over. Setting them carefully in the handheld basket I carry, she gets a funny look on her face before we meander down the frigid aisle.

"Cookie dough? What about you?"

I chuckle as we pause in front of the ice cream, my chest tight as I watch her every movement, enjoying her calm demeanor—enjoying this moment to grow our trust a tiny bit.

"Birthday cake or huckleberry."

Her eyes shine as she grins.

"Me, too, but also sometimes sherbet—"

There's noise at the end of the aisle as a group of said frat boys round the corner, their basket overflowing with alcohol and chips. Alice shrinks in on herself, trying to disappear. I stare them all down just as their eyes chance to rake over her innocent, heavenly body. When they see the possessive, unhinged look in my eyes, they straighten up. Alice tenses, and it's then I realize I've wrapped my hand around her waist and pulled her into my side.

I am about to apologize for touching her without her consent—for the second time tonight, unfortunately—when she goes even more rigid. I follow her line of sight to the end of the aisle as the college boys pass. There stands a man, tall, muscular, but washed-up looking—a visage of the 80's, haggard, gray winding and mingling with the thick golden blond on his head.

His eyes are fiercely blue—the same shade as Alice's.

She whimpers, taking a step away from him, a step that pushes her further into my side, and then I feel her dainty fingers clutching at my jacket, her spindly arm trembling across my lower back. I have a feeling she can feel the imprint of my Glock. Whoever this man is, she knows him, and she's terrified. Terrified enough to cling to me.

I eye him, keeping my face devoid of emotion. His jaw ticks, his sheep-lined denim jacket slipping open slightly as he makes his way toward us, a long bowie knife flashing. I snort, patting Alice's hip, letting her go and moving, keeping my eyes on his approach as I nonchalantly maneuver her to my other side while also opening the freezer door. I'm putting everything I can between her and him.

Her good mood has been zapped from the atmosphere, and it's making me see red. The man draws closer, pretending to inspect frozen breakfast pastries, his eyes still swishing to us every few seconds. I grab a tub of cookie dough, a tub of birthday cake, and a tub of rainbow sherbet for Alice.

Things in the hand basket, Alice safe with me between her and this mystery man, I close the door and move to usher her up front. As soon as my back is turned, he speaks.

"Alice?"

She freezes. After a beat, we both turn, my glare for this man one that should kill him on the spot. His eyes are cold, devoid of emotion, but it is then I see the pieces falling together.

It's her biological father.

"Alice," he breathes, sounding amazed, though I notice the sentiment doesn't touch his eyes. He's just as much a wolf as Tristan and I, but there is one major difference. We were raised to protect and cherish our family. This man? Judging by Alice's fear—by how she flinched away earlier in my office—this man was born to abuse, and everything clicks into an even deeper mold.

I feel Alice shaking, and when I glance down, her lip is trembling, her head swishing back and forth.

"Oh, Alice, honey. It's been…been years. My, you've grown so much. Your mother wouldn't let me see you, and when she married that cock-sucking Russian—"

"Think carefully about your next words, *mertvets*."

His enraged eyes find mine.

"And who the fuck are you, touching my daughter?"

"I am her guardian. Protecting her from men like you," I spit. "Judging by how much she's shaking right now, I'd say she isn't too excited to see such a fucking failure."

He takes a few steps toward us. Alice tenses, but I hold my ground with a sneer.

"Guardian? I saw in the paper that cunt finally died. That means Alice is mine—"

"Not according to the legality of the will, or the fact that you're a felon and aren't fit to raise her."

He fumes, face reddening, and I am beginning to get a taste of what Alice and her mother must have endured before my father fell in love with Anna. For the first time since they met, I am overjoyed; my father saved them from death, for I know men like the one before me, and eventually? Their beatings always go a little too far. I've no doubt Anna or Alice or both would have ended up dead due to domestic violence at some point.

"And you are? You're touching an underage girl, you sick fuck."

"I'm surprised you know the age of your daughter," I say coolly. "But that is besides the point. I suggest you leave before you find out what a *sick fuck* like myself is truly capable of."

It doesn't take the recognition in his eyes long to flame to life. My threat, however veiled, is there, and I know I can back up my shit talking, even without Tristan. Fuck, if Tristan were here, this man would be laid out on the linoleum already. His pale eyes flash back to Alice, who is sniffling—holding back her tears. I hold her even tighter.

He exhales a soft snort, pointing a long, jagged finger at Alice.

"We're not through. That bitch owed me alimony in the divorce—"

"Yes, you are through," I say, taking a threatening step forward, tucking Alice behind me. "And if you threaten her again, I will show you what real fear is, *mudak*."

He turns and leaves with a final sneer.

CHAPTER THREE

JAMESON

Tristan hops over the back of the couch and settles in, reaching for the remote to sift through options. Alice tentatively hovers nearby, ever the nervous, flighty one, especially after the unexpected run-in with her piece of shit father. I'll need to discuss that with Tristan once she's gone to bed. She's so beautiful in her fear and sorrow, so pure, just like a *babochka*—a butterfly. Only, she's yet to metamorphose into herself, held back by the ties of her past.

Eventually, she sinks down into her spot, surprisingly next to Tristan, leaving room for me on her opposite side.

She could've chosen the love seat or the chair, but something about her decision alerts me. That moment we shared in the office and in the frozen pizza section—it wasn't just a level of intensity I've never felt before. It was like a puzzle piece clicking into place. It was the blossoming of trust between us.

I grab a couple of beers from the fridge. The lowlight from under the kitchen cabinets gives off a soft glow, but it barely permeates the darkness streaming in through the massive floor to ceiling window to the left of the living room. Tristan sits closest to the window, and though I think Alice keeps peeking at him, as I meander over, I realize she's nervously glancing at the darkness beyond. Seeing him really did a number on her.

Settling next to Alice, I test the waters and lean across her to hand Tristan his beer. His huff of a snort and the way his lust-glazed eyes meet mine is enough proof; one way or another, she's going to figure out soon—if not tonight—just how deeply we've fallen down this rabbit hole. She's everything we're not. She's everything those other women are also not. She's brilliant, quiet, kind, unique.

Her softness will buff our sharp edges. Her innocence will be our favorite drug. Her smiles will be our reward. We are hopelessly obsessed with her. The thought of her not reciprocating our feelings doesn't matter. She'll eventually learn to trust us with her life, will eventually return feelings of some magnitude.

She is color, brightness, new life, and we are rot, decay, carrion. But the beautiful thing about that? The world needs both to function—just like we need her and she needs us.

As despicable as it sounds, we always get what we want.

Tristan chooses a horror movie—one in which I know there are enough steamy scenes to nearly overshadow the suspense. I want to roll my eyes, but I see what the bastard is doing. We both stretch out, sipping on our hoppy beers as the movie begins. Alice is wrapped up in a throw blanket, her wide blue eyes glued to the screen, her knees up by her chin.

She's tense, nervous between the two of us, chewing her lip and soon her thumbnail. I think I spend the first quarter of the movie watching her, same with Tristan. He eventually slides down with a groan, empty beer cast aside, man-spreading and feigning a stretch to put his arm on the couch behind her. Gritting my teeth, I flash him a glare, but he only smirks back at me over the top of her golden blonde head.

She's always seemed slightly more keen on Tristan. I wonder why that is. It doesn't matter, though; I cannot rip her away from him, just as he cannot rip her away from me. It will be a delicate balance. We've shared before, but the thought of sharing her…

She gasps and then squeaks at a jump scare. Tristan chuckles, eyes swishing to me as he drops his arm around her shoulders and gives a reassuring squeeze. My teeth grind together. Fucker.

Alice tenses at the contact, first peeking at Tristan and then sweeping her round doll eyes to me. She almost looks…bashful. I try to smooth the features of my face, to fucking *smile*, but I feel like it comes out as more of a grimace than anything. Either way, she holds my gaze as Tristan still tenderly holds her shoulder, touching her innocently enough.

Guilt—an unfamiliar emotion—gnaws at me.

But then, a loud thud echoes through the house from somewhere upstairs, and Alice lets out a scream, diving for me, spindly arms jutting out to encircle one of mine. Stunned, I let her hold me as Tristan fights back a chuckle, turning his torso and pressing his chest to her shoulders in a show of his protectiveness as she shivers and hides her face in my arm.

It's probably nothing more than a raccoon. Not five seconds later, another thud sounds, accompanied by the scurrying and scuffling of a fight. The smile that graces my face as Alice clings to me is real.

"Just raccoons," Tristan chuckles. Her head pops up, pink cheeks indicating her embarrassment.

"This too scary for little Alice?" I tease, quirking my brow, trying to keep the mood light after the grocery store incident. Biting her plump lip, she shakes her head, brows drawing together.

"Then what are you so afraid of?" Tristan rasps, leaning in, his cheek pressed to her ear. Eyes locked on mine, her hold on me tightens a degree before she releases me, shaking her head.

"Just…startled me, that's all," she whispers as the movie plays. Tristan backs off, settling into his spot. It takes some time for her breathing to go even again, and her eyes keep flitting to the window, a permanent line between her brows. I want to ease that fear, smooth it away with my lips on her forehead and my arms tight around her.

I also know she needs more time. She has no clue the effect she has on us—likely never will understand it. But baby steps. At least she's here, sandwiched safely between us, more afraid of monsters in the dark than the last of her living relatives.

By the time the movie ends, she's jumpy, prattling off a *thank you* before she disappears into her room for the night. I don't even bother to glance at Tristan as I get up and stomp off to my room, the light beneath her door my beacon. Biting back the impulse to storm in and confess everything, I shove my door open and then slam it closed, locking it for good measure. I barely make it to the shower before I'm stroking my raging hard cock, her name forcing it's way past my clenched teeth.

TRISTAN

"Dinner tonight with Nick Fordson. Should be interesting," Jameson mutters as I pace in front of his desk. His eyes don't bother looking up to me, focused instead on his computer. I only briefly raise my brows in surprise before my thoughts scamper back to this weekend with Alice. She spent most of Sunday out of her room, baking cupcakes and bashfully stammering out if she could please have Thai for dinner.

Fuck.

I know Jameson is right; she's been hurt. By her fucking father. It makes sense now, how tightly she always clung to her mother. Even in Christmas photos, Alice was always holding her hand or a piece of her clothing. It's easy to see when she begins to trust my father; she shifts from standing to the side to beaming proudly and standing between them, his hands protectively on her bony shoulders.

I meander back to the coffee table where the photo album lays open, flipping through the barrage of images again, further cementing what we now understand of her.

Our little butterfly isn't very trusting, but after Saturday, she seems to trust us a tad more. I prefer it that way; I'd rather her be wary of strangers. We know all too well the deplorable things that can happen to her or any other woman. Our father instilled it in us to be gentlemen in that way.

"We're bringing Alice, then," I demand without looking up. Though she's spent most of her time here alone, something about that irks me now. I don't want her to be alone, to be afraid. I'd rather have her with us, safe, getting out of the house and away from the depression we know eats at her.

"Already planned on it," he mutters distractedly. "She has volleyball until five."

"I'll pick her up," I offer quickly, aching for another chance to share some one-on-one time with her. Jameson snorts but nods.

"Fine. Text her so she knows to expect you."

Checking my watch, I hope I don't get her in trouble, but it's noon. That's lunch time for high school, right? Fuck if I remember. I was homeschooled after leaving Russia.

Tristan: Gonna pick you up after practice. We have a dinner to go to.

I set my phone aside, ringer on high, nerves fraying as my knee bounces.

"Jesus, either get the fuck out or take your meds, asshole," Jameson grunts, distracted by me. But I barely hear him as my phone pings.

Alice: Ok, thank you. I'll need a change of clothes...

I type back, thumbs flying over the keyboard.

38

Tristan: Tell me what you need and I'll bring it inside for you.

She details out what she wants and where to find it in her room. Jumping up with a wicked smirk on my face, I turn to leave. Jameson shifts.

"Where are you going?"

"You told me to get out," I say, striding to the door.

"You're far too happy," he growls. I pause at the threshold, turning to grin mischievously at him as I wag my phone.

"Little *babochka* needs an outfit for dinner."

His eyes narrow, his jaw ticking. I love to see the jealousy on his face, so I bask in it for a blissful moment before I turn and leave.

Her room is so tidy, save for her desk. *That* is cluttered with papers and pages of notes, her laptop closed and charging next to a small pile of books. Fuck, she's studious. Jameson is in charge of her schooling and grades, but he's said she's remained a top tier student despite all the shit going on in her life.

Her whole room smells like her, and I take a moment to breathe it in, my cock aching to be free and plunging into her. She smells like flowers—like a field of wildflowers. Not overpowering, just simply there. It's intoxicating, and if I don't get out soon, I'll explode.

I rummage around her closet for the black dress she

told me to find, then sit myself on her pristine bed and rifle through her sock drawer. Back aching, I maneuver my hips to adjust them, but there's something lumpy in her mattress. Annoyed that Jameson probably bought her a fucking cheap one, I toss aside her dress and stand up, lifting the mattress away from the boxspring to see if a spring wiggled out.

Instead, I see a leather-bound book—a journal.

A *diary*.

Before I can stop myself, I snatch it up, sitting back down as I hold the holy grail in my hands. I don't feel one ounce of guilt as I pluck the strings binding it closed and open to the first entry. It's dated over a year ago, to the day her mother and our father died. Heart sinking, my eyes skim her sorrowful prose.

Throughout the entry, she's nothing but grateful for my father and her mother, gushing about how amazing they were, how Vasily taught her to shoot a shotgun and a rifle, how he would take them horseback riding and always included her on their date nights to make her feel welcome and special.

It is the first time I've ever heard this about my father, this soft spot he held for her. He was a good man through and through, and this is evidence of that. I smirk when I come to a part about the funeral, her thoughts on Jameson and I forever inked in her most private diary. But the smile soon slips from my face, my eyes skimming faster and faster, my heart thumping a deep, strong rhythm in my chest.

...they scare me. I know they'd never hurt me. They honestly remind me of Vasily, and now that he's gone...I don't feel safe anymore. What if he finds out? What if he comes back for me? I'll be living with aunt Mary. She can't protect me...

Grinding my teeth, I read on.

...They've changed so much since I last saw them. I feel

40

guilty now for telling mom I was scared of them. I still am,
but I don't think it's anything bad. I think...I think they scare
me because of what they make me feel. No boys at school
look like them. No boys my age are that built, that austere.
They are beautiful. Handsome like the men I read about in
the romance novels I used to sneak from my mom's stash.
They are my step-brothers, though. They shouldn't make me
feel that way.

They shouldn't make me want them. But they do.

For a moment, it feels like the breath in my lungs has
iced over. I cannot breathe. Cannot think a coherent thought
other than an overwhelming sense of exhilaration. She finds
us handsome. She used to read cheesy romance novels and
envision us.

It's taboo. It's forbidden. It's dirty.

And little Alice?

She's curiouser and curiouser.

I flip toward the end of her entries, interest piqued, my
entire body on high alert as my cock throbs in my jeans. I
wonder if she wrote about the movie night with us...

I'm immediately rewarded. The day we picked her up,
she journaled, detailing out how her feelings were still
there, how much it frightened her, how guilty she felt. Her
tone changes, though, on the entry titled:

It's Too Late.

*...Jameson sees me. Like, **really** sees me. No one does,*
no one knows my fears and how to handle them, but in the
office he did—he gave me space but also gave me security.
And when Tristan came in? All I wanted was for them both
to hold me so I could finally fall apart. I can't remember the
last time I had a hug, platonic or not. My horrible dreams
were answered when they wanted to watch a movie with me.
God, how am I so cursed but so lucky? I hope they don't
bring home girls anymore. I think I'd cry myself to sleep if

they did, even if I know being so attracted to them is wrong.

...the movie they picked was a horror. I hate horror, but being sandwiched between them? I couldn't even watch the damn screen. I know how wrong it is, so that's why from here on out, I'll write down every guilty pleasure fantasy I have of them, just to purge it from my system and hopefully move on...

Adjusting my raging boner, my eyes skim faster and faster, my mouth dry with anticipation, my muscles locked, the world around me fading to hues of gray as her scent overwhelms me.

...I want them to be my first. I'm not even remotely sure how that would work or if they'd be into that, but I just want it, damn it. I want Tristan's unbridled wildness. I want Jameson's domination. I've never even come close to sleeping with a guy because my freaking step-brothers have ruined them all for me. I know they are experienced. With looks like those, they have to be—but it doesn't repulse me. If anything, it makes me want them more because they'll know what to do—they'll take care of me.

...God, I feel like such a whore. But I'm committed to this now, diary. I have to purge this and move on. So, here's my first fantasy...

The biting sound of my zipper descending barely registers. Pulling my cock free, the bead of pre-cum on my tip is already trickling down my shaft as I grip it firmly and stroke with a deep groan. I read on, her words my fucking drug.

...I want them both. I want them to take my innocence like in those romance novels. Tristan would probably be my first because he has no patience (does that sound too snooty? God, they are probably more annoyed by me than anything). Anyways, I'd want Tristan, but I'd need Jameson next to me, too, to kiss me, to say sweet things in that growl

of his. And then I'd want him. Whenever I imagine it, I picture Tristan as slow, but unable to contain himself, the sweeter of the two. But when Jameson takes me, I know it would be hard, know he'd push me past my limits and past my fear. I want them to take their turns with me...

I stroke my cock faster and harder as she dives into more detail, all of it tempered with her unrelenting guilt, but all of it so fucking hot.

With a groan and a hiss, my balls tighten and I come all over my hand, rope after rope after fucking rope. I've never come so much in my fucking life. Breathing harsh, my eyes still skimming the pages, my cock begins to stir again immediately after. She says we ruined all other men for her, but she's already ruined all other women for us.

A knock sounds on the door jamb. Growling, I fall back on her bed, not bothering to cast him a glance. I toss him the diary and wallow in my bliss.

Tonight, she's going to be *ours*.

ALICE

I nearly miss the dig, my mind elsewhere, but I dive just in time for the white orb to glance off my wrists and upward to my setter. Ellie creates a perfect frame with her fingers, and Josie—lovingly known as Princess T—spikes it over

43

the net at our coaches. They miss, and our scrimmage team erupts in cheers and claps. Even Aria—a new girl at our school who's been slowly starting to hang out with us—claps her hands from high up in the bleachers. I wonder why she never seems to go home.

Ellie, ever the quiet, meek one, smiles at me and raises her hand for a high five. I slap her hand and grin back. She mostly sticks to herself and her books, but she's honestly the closest friend I have at this school. We're both odd in our own ways—outcasts but allowed to be semi-popular because of our athleticism and *looks*.

Men are pigs.

Josie slaps my ass hard and I yelp, turning to glare at her as she giggles, sweat dotting her luscious dark skin.

"Distracted, Winters?" she jests. I roll my neck as we make our way over to the bench, practice drawing to an end.

"Only because Mr. Bird assigned a shitload of math homework tonight," I say, grabbing my water bottle and pulling the cap up with my teeth. Ellie swigs her water and then elbows me, raising her brows and looking pointedly at something. I follow her line of sight, my blood congealing in my veins.

"Fuck, how did you get so lucky? Can we have a party at your house soon?" Josie says. Tristan stands at the railing of the bleachers, leaned casually against them with a small duffle bag dangling from his tattooed hand. His eyes never stray from me, but there is a small smirk on his lips and mischief in his eyes. God, I hope he didn't get lost in my closet and judge me for how immature some of my clothes are. The giraffe footie pajamas were a spirit week joke, after all.

"Earth to Alice?"

I snap out of it, turning away, but not before another dark figure joins Tristan. I don't even need to wait for my eyes

44

to adjust to know it's Jameson; his presence is an entity of its own. I shiver as I remember how protective he was at the store. During the huddle, I pretty much miss all the information for Thursday night's game, my heart still sprinting in thanks to the sight of them.

I feel so guilty, but I also feel...empowered? Is that the right word? As soon as I'd decided to put pen to paper, to write down all my darkest fantasies about my devilishly handsome step-brothers, I'd felt a sort of catharsis. Imagining what I want them to do to me is as easy as it is difficult; I have no real life experience, so things gleaned from books are my clear go-to's. The rest? It's simply what I imagine they'd be like...in intimate situations. I'm way too much of a coward to ever ask for those things outright. Even if I was in a relationship, I know myself well enough to understand I'd be too embarrassed to be vocal about it.

Plus...they are technically related to me, and even though it's not biological, it still feels dirty—wrong. But that wrongness? It's starting to feel so good. I want to chase that high, that flittering feeling in my chest that dives down between my legs when I know I'm doing something I shouldn't be.

What kind of hole have I dug myself into? I barely know how to make myself feel good. So imagining them taking over, taking control, making me feel good and safe—God, it's the only thing in life I want as much as I want my parents back. I just want to not have to think. I want to feel good and let go. Maybe I should put myself out there more, try to date someone from school, even though that thought immediately repulses me.

I'm torn from my thoughts as we say our cheer and rush to the lockers. I linger back, eyeing Tristan and then Jameson. They look nice; sweaters and jeans. Except nice is an understatement. Their jeans hug their hips, are loose in all the right places and tight across their muscled thighs, the fabric around their zippers stretched slightly—and indication of how well endowed they no doubt are. And those sweaters? Tight across their broad chests and bulging biceps, tapering down looser across their slim waists.

Jameson's eyes rake over me, and I can almost swear they linger on my ass. I blush on cue, but Tristan distracts me as he holds out the duffle.

"For you, *babochka*."

He's smiling, but his grin is…off. It's wider than normal, and I watch as his eyes also trail over my scantily clad butt. I'm wearing my volleyball shorts, so I know they leave little to the imagination. Deciding to tempt fate, I jut my hip out and flash them a small smile of thanks.

I'm rewarded instantly as Jameson covers a cough with his fist and trains his eyes on the ceiling, all while Tristan stares deeply into my eyes, his smirk betraying him. He says something to Jameson in Russian before he steps forward, plucking a strand of hair off my shoulder and pushing it back with the rest of my ponytail. His fingers trail along my collar bone, and I shiver at his fiery touch, some sort of knot pooling in my lower gut. That same feeling I get when I write about them, only with the actual touch? That feeling is amplified a million times.

Jameson says something else, a lighter note to his usually dark-edged voice. Without tearing his eyes from me, Tristan nods.

"*Da*."

Yes. I at least remember one Russian word.

"Give us a tour? We've not been in here before."

I gulp, glancing around. No one's here anymore, and the locker room should be emptying; no one ever stays to shower when there's ones at home. Why would they want a tour? But I am too shy, too nervous to do anything but snap my mouth shut and nod. Maybe they never went to a high school like this back in Russia. I'd be rude not to show them something they're curious to see.

"Umm...follow me?" I say, my words sounding like a question. Tristan dips his chin in a nod, his eyes ignited in that instant, and Jameson's face clouds over, his entire frame tensed. They obey silently as I lead them out of the gym and up the science wing hallways, quietly prattling as I go, sounding like a damn tour guide at a college campus.

"Mr. Finnegan—seriously, that's his name—is like the worst history teacher ever. He just assigned us so much work," I grumble, listening to their footsteps as they follow quietly. We've toured the science and English wings, and I've fallen into an easy sort of banter with myself. It's not so awkward when I pretend I'm with a new student. Make that two new students who are tall, dark, and sinfully handsome. Students that have tattoos and piercing gazes and bodies so muscled they could be models. I ramble over my next words, lost in my fantasies.

One of them snorts behind me, and I turn to glance. Tristan's eyes are relaxed and playful as he dutifully carries my bag. Jameson's hands are shoved in the pockets of his jeans, his sharp eyes narrowing in on everything, seeming to scrutinize even the smudges of ink on the lockers. He spits something to Tristan that I can't understand before he speaks to me.

"We've dinner soon, *babochka*. Where do you change?"

Flames lick up my body and redden my face.

"Umm...back in the locker rooms," I mutter. He nods, and I lead them back through a shortcut. The familiar scent of cloying perfume, sweat, and musty towels is thick in the air outside the locker room, and before I think anything of it, I head inside to grab my things. Only, my heart stops and I whirl, blushing intensely again. They stand dutifully behind me, paused mid-motion as I reach for my bag.

"Thank you for bringing this," I say, my voice catching in my throat. They...were they...*following* me in here? Jameson's eyes darken another few shades while Tristan pulls my change of clothes out of my grasp.

"The tour doesn't stop here, little butterfly."

What?

Did I hear him correctly? I stand dumbfounded, staring at them both as my eyes widen, cheeks flaming. I can change inside a shower stall if they really are that oblivious and want to follow me. Or maybe their culture is different? Pressing my lips together, I'm about to kindly tell them they don't have to come in here when Jameson steps forward, towering over me, crowding my space. Instinctively, I back pedal, but he pushes forward until my shoulders hit the cold cinderblock wall. My eyes stay wide on his chest, palms splayed on the cool surface behind me. Heat radiates off him in waves as he leans over me, placing his own palms on either side of my frame as my mind whirls and tilts.

His presence is intoxicating and stifling, so powerful and dominating that it's all I can do not to shake like a little dog in his shadow. But something else takes root at his proximity; that feeling. The one that tells me I'm doing something so wrong, the feeling that warns me as much as it excites me. Is everyone hardwired this way? To yearn to be bad? To lean into it just so that blissful fire between my thighs has a chance to blossom and engulf me?

He breathes in deep, chest rising slowly before he releases it. When he speaks, I can understand him very clearly this time.

"You're a dirty girl, Alice. But you're lucky."

Confused, I finally chance a peek up at him, his strong jaw coming into view first, scruff dotting his chin. His long black lashes fan out over his bronzed cheeks, his throat bobbing, making his tattoo dance. His eyes though. They are hellfire, a writhing sea of seething, wanton desire. My knees tremble, my breath coming in shaky gasps as his words finally register. Dirty…girl? Lucky?

"L-lucky?" I stammer. The faintest of smirks builds on his full lips as he leans in, face hovering just a few inches from mine. Their scents have become my drug as of late; right now, Jameson smells like his cologne, spicy, fiery, his warm breath minty as it fans over my face. My lips part, my tongue begging to trace his bottom lip. I've never been kissed. Would he indulge that? I almost groan as the thought sends more sparks through my body and down to my core.

"Very lucky to have two big brothers like us, naughty little girl."

His words make my thighs clench, and my cheeks burn as I feel something warm and wet ooze into my underwear. It's happened before when writing about them, or when reading dirty books. But here and now? It feels like his words have unleashed a dam in my panties. Licking my dry lips, I ask the question I know will answer everything.

"Why?" I whisper, voice hushed as Tristan moves just behind Jameson, ever present in the tenseness of this moment. Jameson's smirk broadens, lighting up his face like some sort of menacing demon.

"Because," he pauses, leaning in, his chest brushing against my erect nipples, his hot lips grazing the shell of my ear. "We've wanted to share our little *babochka* for a while now."

CHAPTER FOUR

JAMESON

Her reaction to my words is better than either of us could have ever dreamt. A quiet little whimper of a pleading moan escapes her lips. When I pull away to study her face, her eyes are pinched closed tight, the lids a pale lavender hue, her bottom lip trapped between her pearly teeth. My cock strains against the biting zipper of my jeans, but we cannot fuck her at school. Tristan was annoyed as I'd laid down my rules on our way here until I'd told him why.

Little Alice knows nothing. It's clear by her entries. She's a virgin, she's innocent but naughty—such a beautiful combination. She needs to understand what she wants, what we will do to her. She needs to be prepared mentally, physically. Here and now? It is simply a test, one she is passing with flying colors. We need to see if those dirty thoughts in her mind can be allowed out to play in the light.

Her body is so responsive, her tiny nipples poking the fabric of her sports bra and tank top. Finally, her round blue eyes pop open, pupils blown wide in her lust. She's shifting her hips from side to side, rubbing her thighs together as subtly as she can. One of my hands curls into a fist near her head. She's aroused already. My resolve is gone.

"Would you like us to share you, Alice? Do you want us to fuck you, lick your cunt until you see stars?"

Her gasp turns into a loud mewl, her back arching off the wall as her eyes pinch closed again. I snort softly at her reaction, sounding nonchalant though feeling anything but that. Tristan will get to fuck her first. We won't deviate from what she's written about in her little diary. This poor girl has been through hell and back—she deserves to have her every dark fantasy fulfilled in exactly the way she wants.

I lean in again, tongue darting out to trace the delicate shell of her ear as she shivers and rewards me with a whimpering moan, the light salt of her sweat my new favorite flavor.

"Do you want that, Alice? Because we will give you anything you want. As long as you're our good girl, we'll be your fucking slaves."

Her fingers tick against the wall, as though she's stopping herself from reaching up to grab me. I can feel Tristan shifting behind me, eager, poised and tense and ready to strike at my word. She's too nervous to ask for these things, this I know. She's also terrified of the thought that we will use her and abandon her, fuck with other women. If only she could understand how she's already ruined all other women for us.

But I know it is my job to reassure her. She craves safety and attachment as much as she craves all the wild, dirty things. And we will give her both.

We will be her safety net. We will cherish her, protect her. Give her anything she can conjure up in her beautiful, curious brain. There is no other option for us anymore. Even the thought that she may one day desire to move on doesn't matter; we will ensure she'll never fucking want that.

The subtle nod of her head, the subsequent small cry of desire—of giving in—sends my brain into a fucking frenzy. She slumps suddenly, seeming drained, woozy, but I catch her easily, pinning her languid form to the wall with my body. Every dip and curve, every muscle, every brush of soft flesh against me is something I'll never be able to forget. She melds perfectly to me despite the differences in our sizes.

Already, she's exhausted. I'm sure the overall tenseness of this situation has left her feeling empty. She's admitted so much just with a few nods. And to a woman who's never even had sex, this alone is probably enough for one night, enough of a taste to allow her to wallow in her lust and crave more.

But there's not going to be any stopping anymore.

Bending, I sweep her up into my arms as she gasps. Tristan follows as I walk us fully into the locker room, the space cavernous and abandoned. White and green lockers line the room in rows, and the back of my neck prickles, a sensation I listen to. Being cornered in such a way with no exit is death in our line of business.

Dropping my eyes to hers in a glare, a million scenarios of what could happen to her in a space like this flits through my mind.

"We'll be picking you up from games and practices

inside from now on," I growl. Her light frame tenses, her beautiful eyes wide, but after a moment she melts into me, relaxing as she nods. She understands. Without me having to explain why, she picks up on my cues and obeys. A shiver of excitement tears through me. And I'd thought she was perfect before I read her diary…

Gentle, I settle her back onto her feet, and she teeters before she steadies herself. I promised Tristan his moment with her. If she gets tired, she can sleep on our way to dinner. She'll need it for when we get home tonight.

Setting down her duffle bag on a bench, Tristan plops himself down as well, staring expectantly up at me with that devilish smirk. I roll my eyes. At least he'll involve me in his games versus just making me watch. We'd agreed that after this rendezvous we'd talk this situation over with her, figure out how we factor in. So far (according to her diary) she seems to want both of us present every time.

Alice blinks up at me, cheeks a cherry red, before her eyes swish to Tristan. Wringing her little hands together, she just stands immobile and clearly nervous.

Tristan spreads his arms, gesturing her forward as he also brings his knees apart. Giving me one last glance, she swallows and obeys, tentatively making her way to him as I cross my arms and lean against the lockers. She stops just out of his reach.

"What…what's happening?" she says, her voice small and fraught with nerves. His face softens the same way my heart does. Maybe this is wrong. Maybe she's too young, too naïve, doesn't know what she wants—

"Whatever you want to happen, baby girl," he says lowly, his voice thickening and slipping deeper into our accent. Her eyes flash to me again before back to his. I can only watch like a hungry wolf.

"But…but…I don't understand, how do you—"

"Tristan found your diary," I answer easily. Her head snaps up, face draining of color as Tristan cusses me out in Russian. I roll my eyes at his indignant attitude. We would have had to tell her at some point anyway. He's too scared of losing her; I'm too scared of losing her. No matter what, we cannot lose her to something as stupid as dishonesty.

"Wh-what?" she gasps, backing away far enough that her legs hit the opposite bench.

"You do not have to do anything you don't want," he says, his voice hollow, strained—sorrowful. I understand his perception; he believes she's scared of him, of us, but Tristan often misses subtle cues. Sure, she's nervous, but that glint of lust, the way she continues to press her thighs together, the way her little pink tongue keeps darting out to wet her plump bottom lip—it is clear she's intrigued by the offer.

"Would it help to know we've wanted you for an entire year before now?" I add softly. Tempered for the moment, her breathing calms, her eyes still swishing between us both. After some hesitation, she nods. I can understand how it would be difficult to admit you want to fuck your step-brothers—both of them, at the same time. She's a good girl; saying these things aloud is going to be new, intimidating, but also empowering if she can allow herself that.

"Words, *babochka*," I growl. This elicits a small jump from her, but the veins in her neck throb a little harder.

"Yes…" she says. I smirk. Tristan always was better at playing nice. I wonder how she'll handle his more wild tendencies, the same way I wonder how she'll handle my domination.

"This can be whatever you want, Alice," Tristan says, sounding almost pleading. But as she glances back at him, her demeanor softens. "You deserve a chance to live a life of happiness. And if those fantasies bring you any semblance of happiness, then we will help you get that."

His speech is sincere, earnest, their eyes locked the entire time. After a moment, the tip of her tiny sloped nose reddens, her eyes glass over and water, and a few tears slip loose. She hastily wipes them away as we both tense, resisting the urge to go to her, to comfort her. The last thing we want is for her to feel alone ever again.

"I just..." she sniffles, wiping more fervently at her cheeks as the tears keep coming. "I feel...guilty."

The words finally out, everyone seems to breathe a collective sigh of relief. Tristan snorts, shaking his head, the fluorescent lights glinting on his nose piercing.

"Oh, little Alice. We sure as hell don't feel guilty."

"We understand why you would feel that way, though," I add in, casting my twin a glare that he ignores. Again, she sniffs and wipes at her eyes, staring at her tennis shoes now.

"I...I don't even know what to do...I mean—"

We both move at the same moment, Tristan standing to tower over her, me slipping behind her, my hands clasping her dainty waist. Her rounded ass brushes against my thighs, and my cock surges to life again, the pain almost unbearable now. This little minx has given us blue balls for weeks.

Her sharp intake of breath stirs the stagnant air, and I breathe in deeply her scent of wildflowers and hints of bergamot tea. Biting back the groan clawing its way up my throat, I fix my eyes on my brother. His hands delicately wrap around her hips before he squeezes, a squeak exiting her lips. His eyes flit down, the grin painting his face one I feel in my bones.

I've never seen him so genuinely happy before.

"Can I make you feel good, *babochka*?"

ALICE

His question rattles around in my skull. I feel empty and numb, yet somehow on fire at the same time. They know my ultimate secret. They've read my dirty fantasies. It shouldn't surprise me; the hiding spot for my diary is shitty at best, and something about them tells me they know how to do much more than make a woman feel good.

Even Vasily had his secrets, his job nothing more than a ruse in my mind, but it had never come between him and I, or him and my mom. I trusted her, and so maybe I should trust myself; my gut instinct hasn't been wrong yet. Subconsciously, I lean back into Jameson a little more, the feeling of his warm, sturdy body against mine an absolute comfort. I feel safe with him. Safe between Tristan's arms as well. Being sandwiched between both? If it wasn't for the fire burning between my legs, I could curl up and go to sleep with the truth that nothing would ever get to me with them protecting me.

Their hands dwarf my body, huge mitts that are covered in tattoos and veins and tendons. Hands that are strong, fingers that are nimble and long. I feel more sticky wetness squeeze out of my pussy as I rub my thighs together, that yearning growing so much it is hard to breathe. Is this desire? Is this how they feel with me caged between them?

Because it feels...inexplicable. Amazing, and something in my body is craving *more*.

I go to nod my head before I hear Jameson's voice in my mind, commanding me to use my words. The thought of his deep baritone accented words—of how he quietly bossed me around—has my thighs clenching again. I know my answer in my heart and in my mind, and the tenuous trust I've built with them tells me I'm safe; they won't hurt me. They are Vasily's sons, and he was about as protective as they came. I know his own flesh and blood will be just as adoring and admirable if I just give them that chance. And so, I take the leap of faith, falling down, down, down into the rabbit hole, praying that the guilt eating away at me can fade into the mist of bliss.

"Yes," I whisper, locking eyes with Tristan. His jaw snaps together, his eyes blazing, flicking to Jameson behind me for a moment before they settle back on me. His jaw is more squared, his features more broad, but the difference is subtle. I'm proud that I can pick those small details out.

"I'll be here the entire time, little *babochka*," Jameson whispers in my ear, making me shudder in nervous delight. My heart soars; I need him here. I need his safety, his calm, his authority. At the very same time, I need the dichotomy of his twin; his wild, unrestrained side, his lighter heart, his unequivocal desire. As I stare up into Tristan's stormy gray eyes, I can finally understand the look swirling in those cobalt depths; he wants me. Badly.

Just as badly as I want him.

His fingers skim down to slip into the waistband of my shorts, and my hands jut out, gripping his forearms as a frightened whimper leaves my lips. He stills immediately, his eyes storming, his brows pulling low over his piercing gaze.

"Will it...umm...hurt bad?" I mutter, feeling stupid and

58

naïve and a tad grossed out that my first time having sex will be in a locker room. My friends who have done it have told me the first few times suck, and that even after the initial pain most guys still don't know what they're doing. As much as I trust them both in this moment, I know there's unavoidable aspects.

One of his hands leaves my side, reaching up to gently cup my cheek while Jameson's hands give another reassuring squeeze.

Tristan finally cracks a small smile, breaking the tension. "Not here, *babochka*. We're men, not little boys."

"We know how to make it hurt less when the time comes," Jameson says from behind me, his voice deep and husky. I am relieved and reassured, my body leaning back into his sturdy muscles even more, his warmth verging on fiery. Thank God I won't lose my virginity at my school.

"What...I mean...I've never uhh...well..."

Ugh. If I cannot stop rambling or stuttering, they're going to think me an utter idiot and leave. But Tristan's rough thumb gently strokes my cheek, his smile still present.

"We know this. Your only job now is to relax, to enjoy it. And if you don't," he pauses to shrug, his accent deeper than it has ever been. "Then we stop and get you some food so you don't faint."

His gentle teasing makes me break into a smile as I release a small laugh and some tension, but my heart is still hammering hard enough to shake my entire frame. Is this all real? Or did I get concussed during scrimmage? It has to be a concussion, a vivid dream, right?

Except, those gray eyes staring back at me are much too real for this to be just a dream, and their strong hands holding me up, keeping me warm and safe, they are real, too. Maybe...just maybe...I do deserve to have something good happen in my life. After mom and Vasily died, and then aunt Mary—all within a year—depression has crept into my heart and taken root.

The safety and affection I've found in my depression is the same safety and affection that is being offered to me right here and now. The difference? They will bring me joy, connection, something that is missing in my life. So my decision is even further cemented as I stare longingly into Tristan's eyes.

"I want...I want to feel good, and I want you *both* to be the ones to make me feel good," I say, my voice just a shy whisper. I am answered by his wolfish grin, his nostrils flaring in excitement as his nimble fingers slip beneath the band of my shorts again. Though I am nervous as hell, it's the kind of nervous that is also filled with excitement, like before the roller coaster nose dives down the tracks, or before an airplane takes off. I've no idea what to do or expect, but I trust them both.

Slow, he peels off my tight shorts, catching my thong as well. My eyes slip closed as I shiver in this moment of pure tension. Jameson's grip on me becomes tighter, his body fiery hot as he leans around me, the prickly feel of his scruff making me shudder as he presses his face in the crook of my neck from behind, inhaling deeply.

The tight cloth around my thighs is slowly peeled away, leaving me exposed, the cool air of the locker room creating goosebumps along my flesh. At the same moment, Jameson's tongue languidly darts out, trailing along a pulsing vein in my neck as though tracing the lines to my heart. Tristan stands, suddenly casting me in his dominating shadow, and my eyes blink open.

He raises his hand, and in his fist, my pastel pink thong dangles, the lining sticky and soaked. Jameson growls at the sight, hands wandering up to gently cup the underside of my small breasts. I blush at the sight of my underwear, knowing I'm now naked before my step-brothers from the waist down, knowing they can see how aroused I am.

Tristan's smirk is devious.

"So wet for us, Alice. Do you touch yourself when you write your pretty stories?"

The deep bass of his gravelly voice, coupled with Jameson's teeth scraping against my ear lobe, has me whimpering, shifting from foot to foot to try and create any amount of friction I can.

"Y-yes," I whisper as Jameson's huge hands cover my breasts, engulfing them like tidal waves over the beach. Tristan's smirk disappears, his face darkening like a storm cloud, the depthless black of his pupils blowing wide. In the next second, his palm is cupping my throat with just enough pressure to make me woozy, and his lips descend upon mine with a crash like explosive waves against a rocky shore.

It is electrifying, freeing, to feel his lips on mine, so eager. He's my first kiss, brutal and fast and hungry as his grip on my throat tightens, making me see stars behind my lids. His hot, slick tongue traces the seam of my lips, and I part mine on his silent command. Our tongues swirl, his exploring and claiming every inch of my mouth as Jameson begins to tease and tweak my stiff nipples.

I mewl into Tristan's mouth, these sounds I'm making right now ones I know I've never made before. He rips himself away, leaving me swaying toward him, but Jameson's hand snatches my jaw, turning my face to him so he can steal his own first kiss. I melt into him as soon as our lips meet; he's soft, slow and sensual, his languid motions indicative of how in control he always is; this is my torture, this is his power.

Lurching with a gasp, I turn my face away and down at the feeling of fingers skimming up my bare thighs, but Jameson growls a harsh *Niet* in my ear. I shudder at his command and instead whimper, his hand pushing my face back to his.

Tristan presses kisses to the tops of my thighs, fingers gently smoothing across the fronts to the soft inner skin. Jameson's tongue slips between my lips at the same time he pinches my nipple, hard. I cry out as it sends electric shocks of pleasure down into my belly and pussy. The steady throb between my legs aches as more wetness seeps out.

"She's so fucking wet," Tristan growls. Jameson chuckles darkly into my mouth without breaking our kiss, and somehow that is the most deliciously sexy thing he could ever do. Tristan's fingers wrench my thighs apart sharply, and this time I manage to tear away and peer down at him. He kneels before me like a peasant before a queen, and Jameson's hands slip down to cup the backs of my thighs in a bruising hold. With one upward jerk, he yanks me up and simultaneously spreads my legs wide for Tristan's viewing pleasure. I yelp at the sudden suspension of my body, but Jameson is strong, and Tristan moves forward, his lips level with my weeping cunt.

"What...wait..." I gasp, panting, trying to close my legs against Jameson's unrelenting strength. Tristan's eyes soften, the hard edges of his desire smoothed at my hesitation.

"Are you alright, Alice?" Jameson asks. It's then I realize my nails are digging into the backs of his hands, helping him hold me up and open for his twin. Tristan's eyes never leave mine despite me being bared to him for the first time.

"I...I need to shower..." I whisper, reddening. My friends who've had sex often regale me with stories of oral sex, saying it's way better than actual sex. Knowing Tristan aims to use his mouth, I can't help but to be self conscious. They both answer my worries with deep chuckles, but Tristan is the one to speak.

"Oh *babochka*," he says with a shake of his head, leaning in closer to where I can feel myself dripping. His palms splay on the insides of my thighs, pushing me even farther apart. "I've waited for this for too long to give a fuck about that."

And then, with our eyes locked, with his twin holding me open wide for him, he darts his tongue out before sucking my clit into his mouth. I throw my head back with a cry, my skull crashing to Jameson's shoulder as Tristan sucks and flicks his tongue over my swollen bud. My orgasm doesn't hesitate, but instead rips through me so fast and so hard that I turn my face toward Jameson's neck and bite down at his shoulder junction, trying in vain to hold the scream of ecstasy between my teeth.

But Tristan doesn't stop, even when I grow sensitive. I moan and cry out, but he only slows the strokes of his tongue, allowing me to adjust without flinching away. Jameson groans behind me.

"You're so beautiful, *babochka*, perfect. You're such a good girl."

His words amp me up again. I never knew I would enjoy hearing praise so much, but it makes me feel adored and beautiful. All things I've always wanted from the men in my life—things that were hard to come by until my mom met Vasily.

I'm distracted by the building of my next climax, but then I feel it; Tristan swirling his middle finger in the wetness at my entrance. My pussy flutters and then clenches. He removes his mouth from me, instead slowly inching his long middle finger into me. I whimper as I watch him, the stretch nothing with how wet I am.

"You want more, baby girl?" he asks as he withdraws his finger before slowly pushing it back in. My mind in a state of such arousal, I am moaning as I nod, the thought of being filled making me animalistic in my fiery need. I can't even manage to use my words before Jameson nearly makes me come again with what he says.

"Be a good girl and take his fingers in your cunt, Alice. I want to watch you come again."

Tristan licks my slick off his lips before he pushes two fingers into me. The stretch is tighter this time but still nothing painful; if anything, I am enjoying the threat of pain right now, for everything feels intensely heightened. He works his fingers to a certain point before stopping, saying something to Jameson in Russian, who responds simply and quickly.

"*Niet.*"

With a smirk, Tristan's tongue traces my folds before dancing over my clit again. That, coupled with his fingers thrusting shallowly in and out of me, my next orgasm builds at a deep, alarming rate.

"Ahh, ahh!" I cry, gripping Jameson so hard I know he'll have bruises.

"Good girl, such a good girl, come hard for us."

My climax sweeps through me from head to toe, my legs shaking, my toes pointed in my shoes and my muscles locked with the force of its wrath, and something warm spurts out of me. Panicking but too exhausted from those two orgasms, I can only slump with a whimper in Jameson's arms.

"Fuck me, she's a—"

Jameson cuts him off in Russian.

"*Da,*" Tristan says, sounding as dreamy as I feel at this moment.

"Did I...did I pee?" I hedge with a pant, so embarrassed and mortified. I keep my eyes closed, but their chuckles make me peek one lid open. Tristan is shaking his head, his smile so pure and genuine and *happy* it makes my heart clench. He leans in, pressing a kiss to my exposed, ticklish stomach. I wriggle with a small laugh as I attempt to pull away, but his heavy hands on my hips and Jameson still holding me up keeps me in place.

"No, baby. You squirted."

"Umm…what?" I say, feeling so naïve and clueless. His smile isn't patronizing, and he presses a kiss to my inner thigh.

"When you came, you released more fluids. Fucking sexy as hell."

I gulp, still embarrassed, having never heard of something like this before. But if they like it, then I suppose it's a good thing.

"We'll have to wait for my turn," Jameson says lowly behind me before bending to press his lips to the side of my neck. I shiver and curl in on myself, wanting nothing more than to snuggle up next to them both and sleep for an entire day, basking in how perfect this moment feels. He pulls his mouth away. "Get dressed for dinner, *babochka*. But your panties stay with me."

TRISTAN

I am thankful Jameson drives. Alice sits in the front passenger seat, and I cannot take my fucking eyes off her if I wanted to. Her cheeks seem permanently flushed with arousal and her slight embarrassment. She fussed over her hair in the locker room, smoothing it back into a sleek, high ponytail that showcases the bone structure of her flawless face.

The taste of her still lingers on my tongue. Musky, soft, a hint of sweetness. My cock strains against the rough fabric of my jeans, aching to thrust into her tight, virgin pussy as soon as I fucking can. She is perfect. This situation is perfect. She wants us, and we want her, and all of our dirty fucking fantasies are coming to life because we all have a common purpose, now, and the possibilities are endless.

"What's this dinner?" Comes her sweet voice from the front. She shifts in her seat, her black dress tight, hugging her every subtle curve, ending mid-thigh. I can tell Jameson isn't happy about how little it leaves to the imagination, but he has nothing to worry about; with both of us around and acutely aware of her very move, nothing will ever happen to her. She is ours, and we protect what's ours.

"For our...associate. Mr. Fordson."

Jameson is careful not to reveal too much, but Alice is sharp; I can tell as she glances at Jameson and frowns at the side of his face that she is concerned. I would quell her fears, but Jameson and I differ on our view of this situation; do we tell her what we really do? Arm her with the truth? Or keep her locked away from that side of our world until we're sure she won't run to the police or her case worker?

I believe she is mature enough, clearly. If she wants to take our cocks, she's of sound enough mind to know we're in the mafia. Jameson I suspect wants to preserve as much of her innocence as possible.

"You look beautiful," he tacks on, his voice so low I almost miss it. Her face whips to stare at him again, her eyes widening and glossing over. She responds exceptionally well to compliments, to praise. She deserves it. Though that is more Jameson's kink, it is something I can do for her, especially since it's the honest fucking truth. She is simply stunning, a classic, age-old type of beauty.

"Thank you," she whispers demurely back, her eyes falling to his hand on the gear shift as a new blush paints her cheeks. I roll my eyes. There is bound to be some jealousy at some point in any type of poly relationship. Thinking otherwise sets you up for disaster. It's learning how to cope, how to carve out time individually and together to ensure everyone feels secure. These are things Alice will have no notion of, things Jameson and I will have to help her with.

Although I feel jealousy more potently than he does, he's often pointed out we are literally identical. If she's lusting after my twin, she's obviously lusting after me as well. The rest of the ride is quiet, clear that all of us are lost in the haze of this massive shift in our lives. Everything is cast aside as Jameson turns off the darkened, evergreen lined highway and to the road leading to the Fordson's gate. It is open, but a man in a black suit stands guard. Jameson rolls down the window, the two nodding in acknowledgment before he proceeds.

Their home is extravagant, sprawling, the circular driveway with the fountain smack in the middle fucking ostentatious as hell. But I like Nick, his brother Jonah. The two Fordson boys are well on their way to taking over their father's empire, and being on their side is a choice our father, grandfather—hell, even our great-grandfather—had already made for us.

With our similar goals, it is a no-brainer. It helps that I can actually stand Nick, for there are numerous, lower-totem families that are as slimy and sick as they fucking come. I'll be making sure Alice stays clear of any brushes with the Baptiste's or Nelson's.

Jameson pulls to a stop but leaves his car running, a valet coming around to open Alice's door. I hop out, eyes burning as Alice stands and smooths down her little black dress, her strappy heels too high for my taste. If we were home alone, I'd make her strut around in those naked, just to watch the way her pert little ass would jiggle.

The man holds out his hand to her as she teeters on the gravel, his eyes raking over her young body. My teeth gnash together as I shove his hand away, taking hers in my own, threading her arm through mine to hold her steady.

"Apologies, sir," the man says. I ignore him as Jameson snorts.

"Best behavior," he reminds me in Russian. I quirk my brow at him as we mount the steps, his eyes traveling down to Alice's ass.

"You're one to talk," I growl back. Alice slows her steps before we enter the foyer, and I glance down at her in slight concern.

"What is this dinner about?" she asks, the unease in her gaze making so many emotions swirl in my chest. I want to soothe her fear, want to spread her pretty thighs and bury my face in her cunt again and again and again until she begs me to stop.

She's no idea what she's in for once we get home. Jameson better let her stay home from school tomorrow. She'll need the rest.

"To catch up and ensure our…ideals still align," I explain, albeit cryptically. Chewing her pinkish lip, she nods, her hold on me tightening before she glances at Jameson next to her. Gentle, he presses his fingertips to her lower back, bending to whisper something in her ear that I know he intends for me to catch.

"We won't leave your side, *babochka*. And when Tristan drives us home, I'll show you why I kept your panties."

68

A hum of a moan escapes her lips as I chuckle and bring us over the threshold and into the immaculate mansion.

The foyer is bustling with people, glasses of champagne and wine clinking, Janine Fordson like an angel from heaven above whisking around to ensure everything is as perfect as she is. Growing up, everyone gave Nick shit for how fucking hot his mom is. Jameson learned to keep his mouth shut, but I never did. I think I still have a scar on my ribs from him stabbing me for making a MILF joke one time.

The behemoth comes into striking view, standing in slacks and a white dress shirt, the sleeves rolled up his forearms, exposing his grandfather's priceless watch—an heirloom from when all our great-grandfather's made their first business transaction. Jameson has ours locked in the safe at home.

Nick Fordson is a fucking beast; almost seven feet tall, every inch of him rippling in muscle, his dark hair making his eery blue eyes look like electric neon signs in a bar. But that's not what everyone notices despite how out of place he is in a crowd. No, it's the scars that run diagonally across his face that cause people to pause, to stare, for kids to curl into their mother's sides in fear. They are deep, purple in some spots, one running across his left cheek, another splitting his left eyebrow, a third across his forehead.

It is a macabre piece of artwork permanently etched onto his face. And he doesn't take kindly to anyone staring at them. The story of how he got them circulates our world like the most rich gossip. I lean down to Alice's ear, about to give her fair warning, when she gasps and frees herself, tugging away and almost running to Nick.

Jameson and I share a confused glance before we follow her trajectory, apprehensive for what she may say. But she only pauses off to his side, a young girl near her age standing there in a beautiful yellow dress, looking lost and nervous. I hold my hand up, pressing against Jameson's chest to keep him planted, to allow Alice a chance to speak with this girl

"Who is it?" he asks, voice low. Stumped, I give a shrug as the girls' faces brighten, as they smile and chatter amongst themselves. It is then I feel my skin prickle, as though I'm being watched. My eyes flick to Nick, who's glaring at me.

"Fuck," I hiss as he peels away from his father and draws nearer to us. My side throbs in memory of how painful his retribution is.

"Fordson," Jameson says, curt, cautious but polite. Nick glares down at us.

"The Stefanov brothers. My condolences about your father. I was…indisposed. I'm sorry I couldn't make his funeral," he says, voice deep and gravelly. Jameson nods.

"Thank you. It's…been difficult, but we're learning to manage."

"Good, good," he says distractedly, glancing over his shoulder at the girls as Alice shows her apparent friend something on her phone. I cannot help but let my eyes wander all over her perfect body, the way her dress hugs her thighs and ass, the way her braless breasts are like precise tear drops, nipples hard in the drafty foyer.

"Our step-sister, Alice. We've just taken her into our custody," Jameson explains, likely so we don't look like creeps. It'd be worse if we both were attracted to her friend as well, but we're not; Alice is unique, her beauty classic, her maturity something she's always encompassed. The twelve-year gap in our ages means little when the heart you love feels so closely tied to your own.

I cough, covering it barely with my fist as the thought hits me fucking hard.

Love.

Do I really love her? We've known her for long enough,

have lusted after her for a year, but does that equate to love? I wouldn't know; it's not an emotion I've found myself capable of before.

Nick's burning stare flashing back to us has my thoughts scattering. Something akin to a hurricane brews in his gaze. He swallows hard.

"Keep an eye on her. I'm assuming she attends Seattle Prep with Ellie."

"And who would Ellie be to you?" I ask, being a smart ass. His brows drop low over his eyes in vehement warning, and though most would back down, I'm a glutton for punishment.

"A very bright young woman who will not be gawked at," he hisses, protective. I glance at Jameson.

"He's not fucking her, if that's what you're wondering," Jameson growls in Russian, though we both know Nick can catch most of it. The beast's eyes soften as a frown graces his lips.

"No. But she is…" he pauses, as though the word is difficult for him to say for whatever reason. "She is very important. She just doesn't know it yet."

CHAPTER FIVE

ALICE

Dinner is an interesting affair, made somewhat better because Ellie sits by me the entire time. Her father is also associated with this mysterious Mr. Fordson, but at least I have someone my age, someone I am comfortable with. It feels like everyone around me knows; they know Jameson and Tristan are something akin to my taboo lovers (which feels weird calling them that), and it feels like everyone can read the glaring sign on my forehead: GUILTY.

Of course I feel guilty for what we'd done in the locker rooms. I feel dirty, wrong, as though society will shun me.

What if I get kicked out of school? What if they go to jail? I'm the legal age of consent, but these fears are gnawing away at the pit of my stomach.

As soon as my eyes find either of theirs, my fears and my guilt seem to fade away, replaced instead by calm, a type of peace that feels unreal and therefore too good to be true. Why they make me feel this way, I don't quite understand yet. Maybe it's the way Tristan's eyes narrow mischievously when they meet mine. Maybe it's the way Jameson broods as he stares at me, his mask rigid and unreadable, but the subtle hints of his desire are there if I look closely enough. They take turns, too. If one moves away, the other draws closer. If my back is exposed, one will gently steer me or give a small reassuring touch that sends fire through my veins.

After experiencing two earth shattering orgasms back to back, you'd think I was tired, sated—but all I want is more.

Sitting through dinner is torture. I'm still wet, growing wetter whenever Tristan licks his lips, whenever Jameson's fingers trail up my thigh beneath the table. By the time we are in the car heading home, my body is buzzing with excitement, my guilt squashed under my own heel. I should be able to do whatever makes me feel good, within reason. I still have morals.

Kinda.

Tristan drives, Jameson occupying the captain's chair next to mine. They converse lowly in Russian as dark trees blur by and we head east toward Seattle. I know we have a little bit of a drive until we make it home, and so as their low voices waver to me through the quiet cabin of the car, I daydream, forehead pressed to the cold window.

I conjure up more ideas of what I want them to do to me. Having Jameson hold me off the ground and spread open for Tristan was probably one of the hottest things to ever happen to literally anyone. Watching Tristan's tongue flick against my clit before sucking it roughly between his lips? I rub my thighs together at the fiery memory, my nipples pebbling in my dress until they ache to be sucked, too. I've never been able to give myself orgasms of that magnitude before. I've never even fingered myself. I never really knew if it would feel good or not, so I never tried.

Now I know, and the thought excites me even more.

"We must speak, Alice," Jameson says quietly. Sitting straighter, I adjust my seatbelt and nod, glancing over at him. His dark brows are heavily slanted over his brooding eyes. I think I know what kind of talk they want to have with me, and my heart begins to race out of nervousness. Are they about to force my hand? Come up with some impossible rule because they realize after that one encounter that they really don't want this? Are they going to laugh at me and call me a freak for my fantasies?

"We care very much about you. We have for many years," Jameson says. I swallow hard. He'll be the one to give this speech because that's just how he is; concise, cut and dry and to the point. I keep my hands folded tightly in my lap to hide their shaking.

"We will not mince words with you. Of course we desire you sexually. I think you understand the repercussions should anyone find out while you're still in school, *da*?"

I nod mutely, feeling the sober air of the atmosphere, understanding what it is he's confirming with me.

"Good. The rest…" he pauses, frowning ahead before his eyes slide back to me. "There is much you will learn on your own, much we will be able to teach you. But with that comes rules, understand?"

Again, I nod.

"Safe, sane, sober, consensual," he says, ticking off the four points on his long fingers. I push the thought of him pinching my nipples away and try to focus. "Whatever you want us to do and whatever ideas we might present to you will be safe."

"Even if they don't seem safe," Tristan butts in. Jameson growls something at him but expands on that.

"I think he's speaking about a particular fantasy of yours, one we will discuss after tonight."

My stomach immediately knots up; I think I know which one. I'd been hoping they hadn't read that far…

"Another aspect of safe is…well…" he trails off, but Tristan is quick to pipe up.

"We're clean. Got tested last week."

I immediately blush, biting my lip as Jameson shifts, commanding my attention with his mercurial eyes.

"We're assuming you are as well," he says as I nod quickly, eyes wide. He smiles softly. "But there is the aspect of birth control—"

"I'm on it," I rush out, palms feeling clammy. Aunt Mary put me on it last year for my acne. He shuts his mouth, eyes softening slightly as he nods. I gather that as men, they don't really feel like talking in-depth about my cycle, which I am totally alright with. With a sigh, he plunges ahead.

"Next is sane. Meaning we will never attempt something that could permanently harm you. Sober—"

"I'm not old enough to drink," I mumble, trying to tease him gently. After a moment, he smirks.

"No, *babochka*, but I'm sure my counterpart has no issue sneaking you whatever booze you'd like."

"She's old enough for our cocks, she's old enough for good vodka, *mudak*."

I can't help but giggle and burn bright red at the same time. Jameson growls something back at him, but Tristan just chuckles. They quiet, and the mood in the car shifts to a more serious note.

"Last, consensual. We will never do anything to you that you do not want, Alice, you understand that, right?"

His words and the way he stares deeply into my eyes through the darkness makes me feel so warm, so cherished. I know intrinsically they would never harm me like that. But to have that extra added layer of comfort? It means a lot to me. I know I'm not strong physically, know they obviously are. They could easily take advantage of that, but they wouldn't.

"Yes," I say, my voice weak and strained.

"Do you need a safe word tonight?" he asks lowly. The car jerks to the left a little, Tristan overcorrecting because he'd been listening more to us than paying attention to the road. It almost makes me smile.

"I…don't know? What would that do?"

I've heard my friends talk about it, but I've never cared much to figure out what a safe word really is. Part of me begins to wonder if I am too young, too dumb. But another part of me knows I will learn this someday either way. And I'd much rather it be with them, two men I want, men I trust.

"It means if you say it, we stop everything immediately because you're at your limit," Tristan says. I chew my lip in thought. What are my limits even? I guess I'll figure them out as we go, which I think is best for me.

"Oh…umm…maybe…sherbet?"

Jameson glances at Tristan as they chuckle. I sink further in my seat at this, but I don't feel like they're mocking me; it feels like they find my choice endearing somehow. The air in the car changes to a more sober note again.

"You should also understand our likes. We don't want to frighten you in the moment, you know?" Jameson says.

His accent is so rich and velvety right now. It makes me quiver with desire. Desire to hear him tell me what a good girl I am again.

"For instance," Tristan says proudly. "I like it fucking dirty and rough. I'll choke you, spit on you, bite you, make you come even when you beg for me to stop."

My eyes bulge out of my skull at his brash words, but the images he paints in my mind are works of art; me sweaty and used, exhausted as his massive hand encircles my throat and he pumps into me.

"And me, *babochka*," Jameson says, tearing my attention away from my fantasy. "I like to tie you up so you cannot move, so your legs are spread and I can see how wet you get for me when I slap your little cunt, when you take your punishments like a good girl."

Now my heart is racing, the seatbelt restraining me like how he wants to tie me up. His eyes are malicious, glinting like a pale silver fish in the depths of a black lake. He unbuckles, drawing closer to me as his hand dives into his pocket and produces my pink panties.

"This is for you, brother," he says, though his eyes never leave mine.

"Tell me," Tristan growls.

"Your dirty girl needs to keep it down while we drive. We can't have her screaming and distracting you."

Tristan's answering chuckle is menacing. My eyes flit between the back of his head and the underwear in Jameson's huge hand. He tsk's at me, and my wide eyes fly to his as my pussy aches, my clit begging for attention.

"Spread your legs for me, beautiful girl," he says, his voice like a thunderstorm, his pupils wide. Slow, I scoot down in the chair to more easily spread my legs as wide as they can go. His unwavering eyes watch my every move with such scrutiny I'm unintentionally tense and praying I've done a good enough job to hear him tell me so.

I'm rewarded with the slight uptick of his lips and his

next words.

"Such a good listener, *babochka*. Now open your mouth nice and wide for me."

I'm catching on to what is going to happen. If I wasn't in this situation, I'd find it gross, but knowing how much it is going to turn Tristan on? Knowing how I'll be praised and made to feel good for obeying? Something in my mind clicks into place, shutting everything else off. It is strange—new—but I love it. I am still Alice, but I am their good girl. The only thing in my mind is how to please them, how to make them squirm like they make me writhe. And right now, obedience seems to be doing it for all of us.

This feeling is freeing, cathartic. I don't have to think. I don't have to put on a fake smile. I don't have to pretend I haven't been severely depressed for an entire year because everyone I love keeps dying. I have them now. A slight bright spot at the end of the blackest tunnel, growing wider as I scramble to catch it, to chase it. I feel like a butterfly about to escape its chrysalis after months spent in the smothering darkness; beautiful and free and strong.

I open my mouth wide, Jameson's eyes glowing through the dark car. I keep my eyes on his, pinned to the seat by his gaze, completely surrendered and trusting of him in this moment. My body feels like pliable dough; he can do with me what he pleases, but he's still chivalrous enough to ask.

Leaning in, his lips brush my ear.

"Are you sure, Alice?"

I nod before he's even pulled away, sticking out my tongue as far as it will go to entice him further as the ache between my legs grows more fervent, as I feel my wetness slipping down my slick skin. He lets out a growl at the sight and fists my ponytail, yanking backward until I'm gaping up at him with a whimper. He leans in, tongue darting out to lick mine, sending tingles through my body. When he pulls away, the lacy cloth is at my lips, pushing past my teeth and settling on my tongue. Once all the fabric is in, he traces a finger down my puffed cheek as I whimper.

"Such a good fucking girl, Alice. You're so beautiful," he murmurs against me as I whine, my chest rising and falling rapidly as I ache to pull my thighs together. Unable to resist, I close my legs, but his eyes catch the movement, and he wrenches me apart with his strong hands. Before I know it, he's yanked my dress up so the cloth barely covers my pussy, and his palm strikes the inside of my thigh.

I yelp at the sting, lurching forward as much as the seatbelt will allow.

"If I say spread your legs, you keep them open, *da*?"

Whimpering, I nod quickly, hands clutching the armrests.

"When you play with yourself, do you put your fingers here, Alice?" he asks, thumb pressing hard against my slippery clit. I moan on contact, the sound garbled and high pitched as electric waves of the utmost pleasure tingle through me and make my pussy clench and beg for more, the sting of his palm striking my skin fading. I nod assent. Slow, with his pointer finger, he drags it down to my core where I'm slick with arousal. Gentle, he probes my entrance, teasing me as my body begs for more.

"Here?" he whispers. This time, I shake my head. He relays something to Tristan that I don't understand, but his attention is soon on me again.

"Do you want us tonight, Alice? I need you to be honest. We can wait if you're not ready."

He seems to already know my answer because he's smirking as he swirls his finger in me. I've wanted them for a while now. I don't want to wait any longer. My nod is quick and sure. His free hand comes up to cup my cheek, and I lean into his warmth, rubbing my face against his palm.

"I'm going to break your hymen, then, *babochka*, and when we get home you'll be ready to take our cocks."

His words are as reassuring as they are igniting, and my eyes roll back as my head thuds against the back of my seat. Keeping his hand on my cheek, he withdraws his finger and then inserts two, thrusting shallowly to stretch me before he probes something tender. My eyes open to swish between his fervently, air rasping in through my teeth and lacy panties. He gives me the softest smile I have ever seen, one full of longing and something else, something deep and loving. He smooths his palm over my cheek, brushing a few hairs away.

He thrusts a little more, and I feel a slight pinch and burn at the deeper foreign intrusion, but the pain is minimal.

"Look down. See how deep my fingers are in your tight little cunt, Alice."

Raggedly breathing, I obey, my eyes widening as I see his thumb, pinky, and ring finger, the other two disappeared to the hilt. As he withdraws slowly, I can see the sheen on his fingers, showing me how wet I am.

"Did you tell her how we'll kill any fucker that ever tries to get anywhere near her?" Tristan seethes from the front seat. His sentiment makes me moan. Jameson chuckles.

"Noted, brother. You should see what a good girl she's being."

Tristan grows silent, but I can almost feel how desperate he is just by how robotically he's driving.

Jameson's thumb rubs soft, slow circles around my clit in time with his deep, gentle thrusting. I feel like he's opening me up, preparing me in the most erotic way possible for what's to come. His teeth nip at my ear as he leans in.

"Watch me make you gush all over my fingers, and then you're going to clean it up, yes?"

I whine against the panties in my mouth and nod, my

nails now clawing into the armrests, my thighs quivering with each pump of his fingers. Deep within me, I can feel it tightening, can feel my stomach knotted up in preparation for the tidal wave this orgasm is going to be. My whines grow louder, closer together, and his thrusts become rougher, his thumb circling faster and faster. The wet, sucking sounds of his fingers in my pussy echoes in the car, and I watch it all, tensing as he crooks his two fingers deep within me.

I can't breathe, or make sense of time or space. All I can do is watch on the precipice of a cliff as he fingers me, as my legs shake, as my belly clenches and my cunt ripples and clamps down on his fingers greedily. My climax makes me scream against the cloth in my mouth, but I still obey, watching as I coat his fingers and wide palm in a gush of fluids. He groans in my ear as I cry and wither around him, stray hairs plastering to my sticky forehead. I slump back with a whimper, my body slack as he withdraws his fingers. I feel his other hand at my mouth, tugging my panties out, before pressing his two, hot, slick fingers to my lips.

With a moan, without realizing what I am doing, I grab his wrist and force his fingers into my mouth, tasting myself on him as I suck him clean and lick his palm like a ravenous animal.

"Fuck, I'm so proud of you, my good little slut."

His words only make me suck his fingers harder, my tongue flicking between them, his hungry eyes locked on mine. I am whining as he pulls away, but he smooths his other hand over the top of my head, calming me. Everyone is quiet, basking in the eroticism of this moment. Finally, I manage to blink my droopy eyes open to find Jameson already staring down at me, his hand still brushing over my cheek soothingly. I am still clutching his wrist, and I blush but smile, coming out of my daze, coming back into my body—into myself.

"What'd you do to me?" I mumble, turning my smile up to him. He returns it, his own soft grin a rare sight.

"What we'll do to you for the rest of your life. Make you feel like the princess you are."

JAMESON

I stare down into Alice's round ocean eyes. Even through the darkness, I can still see how they shine just for us, how sated and fulfilled she is. She is so ethereal, so beautiful that it makes my heart ache for the first time in years. Tristan's always been too flighty for love, even though I know he loves her. It is clear by how he looks at her; he's never been this way with another woman.

Me? I've loved before. It was a brief, year-long stint with a woman from our world—and she'd gutted me by leaving me for another man. I'd sworn off even the thought of dating until I'd seen Alice at the funeral last year, saw how she'd grown into such an elegant, graceful beauty.

Until I saw the pain in her eyes and knew I'd stop at nothing to fix it, to comfort her, to bring just one smile to her plush pink lips.

She nuzzles my palm with her cheek, eyes closing, brows pinching as a soft sigh leaves her lips. Gently, I speak to Tristan as she dozes, the memory of her cunt gripping my fingers greedily, of her hot mouth sucking them clean afterwards, giving me a raging hard on.

"She's tired," I say softly in Russian.

"One of her fantasies," he quips back. I roll my eyes. He wants her tonight, consequences be damned. I want her to be physically well, but I cannot deny how badly I am aching to bury myself in her.

Something she wrote briefly about in her diary that she wants to try is for us to use her—literally use her, whether she's awake, asleep—she wrote she didn't care. I can already see by her reactions just moments ago that she is a natural submissive; she slipped into a completely different headspace from the innocent, meek Alice we know and turned into a voracious animal in heat. Fucking sexy vixen.

But for as hot as that is, the other part of me wonders why she has these fantasies, why she wants to be used, commanded, praised. She wrote she was afraid of someone coming after her, and after seeing her biological father at the store, after watching their tense interaction, I think I have an idea of who it is.

"She's afraid of her real father," I whisper to Tristan. He growls low in his throat as Alice's warm breath tickles my palm. She's fast asleep.

"Then we kill the fucker."

"Not that easy," I snort. Killing her father would likely still hurt her despite whatever he's done. But it does give me some insight into her kinks. The thought that maybe he hurt her at some point enrages me, but we won't know unless she tells us. Until then, if we allow her fantasies to come to life in a safe environment, she may do just that.

And we may just be pushed over the edge to the point we...rectify that.

We soon pull into the garage, and I gently lift Alice out and bring her inside. I can feel Tristan's unbridled, jittery desire as I walk her to the couch and lay her down, pulling her favorite knit blanket over her. Before I can admonish him and tell him to let her have some time to adjust, he's kicking off his shoes, slipping his belt through its loops, and discarding his shirt.

"Seriously?" I hiss. He smirks and shrugs, his inked chest and pierced nipples on display as he slips behind her on the couch, pulling her slack body into his, wrapping her up in his arms. The sight makes jealousy flair for a moment before calmness takes root. Tristan is the only person in this world I'd trust her with, and as a soft smile paints her lips, I know she feels that safety as well.

I'm about to leave them to it when Alice's little hand snaps out, reaching for me and brushing against my thigh. Tristan chuckles up at me before burying his face in the crook of her neck.

"You can't leave me, remember?" she whispers, blinking tiredly up at me as her smile grows. My body ignites in flames as I turn and sink to my knees by her face, reaching out to cup her cheek.

"You're sure you're ready? Not too tired? Or sore?"

Pressing her lips together, she pauses to roll her shoulder and glance at a grinning Tristan, eyes widening slightly as she takes in his nude torso. When she turns her gaze back to me, a steely glint has entered her big blue eyes. She pushes herself up into a sitting position.

"I...I want to see you both..."

My eyes catch Tristan's. We know exactly what she means without her having to fully ask the question. He shifts and stands, as do I, towering over her as she sits expectantly on the couch, fire in her eyes despite how tired she really is. I would glance at Tristan, but judging by the way her eyes widen, I already know he's showcasing his cock proudly for her. Feeling left out, I narrow my eyes and begin to strip, something akin to nervousness fluttering in my chest.

Tristan and I are both covered from head to toe in tattoos. He sports piercings through his nipples and a hoop in his nose. My body mods, however...they may frighten her a little. It's something I never thought I'd be self conscious about, mostly because the women we usually fuck could be porn stars and are used to seeing rare things.

Alice, though? I doubt she has any idea these types of modifications could exist. I strip down until I'm in my boxers, my cock half-hard and aching at all the lack of attention I've received.

She eyes us both, standing before her in nothing but shorts. Tristan glances at me, self-assured, cocky as ever. I'd roll my eyes if I wasn't apprehensive. Alice clears her throat, her eyes on mine, a note of mischief to her gaze.

"May...may I?" she whispers, hand tentatively outstretched. Fuck. How can I deny her when she's staring up at me with mussed hair and moist pink lips? After my fingers were just deep within her cunt? When she was such a good girl cleaning up her mess?

Slow, smirking, I peel my boxers off, allowing my now fully erect cock to spring free. Her eyes give her away as they widen, her lips parting. Regardless if she finds this strange or weird, she'll learn to appreciate the pain I went through to give her the utmost pleasure. I grip my cock, stroking slowly, tightening my grip as I get to the top and pre-cum leaks out of my tip.

"Like what you see, *babochka*?"

CHAPTER SIX

ALICE

Holy. Shit.

They stand before me, one fully naked, one almost naked. Both their bodies are covered in dark, intricate and beautiful ink that accentuates every dip and curve of their delicious muscles. Tristan's nipples are pierced by barbells—something I never thought I'd find as sexy as it is on him. I have to resist the urge to run my tongue along the metal.

But the real shock? It is Jameson's apprehension, the way his eyes had gone tight when I'd asked him to strip.

He's nervous about something, but now, as he grips his huge, thick cock, I can see why.

I've only ever seen a dick on a porn that I secretly watched last year when I realized I had a crush on them but couldn't get those dirty thoughts out of my head. The one I'd seen in the short movie had been long and thin. Jameson's (and clearly Tristan's) is just as long but insanely thick.

And through the purplish head is a barbell piercing that makes my insides squirm with desire. My pussy clenches, more arousal flooding me. When my eyes travel down his shaft, watching as he slowly strokes it right in front of my face, I notice something even more peculiar.

Round lumps beneath the skin of his shaft—nodules dotting the underside and top in some sort of pattern. It's then I realize this isn't by accident, but rather by design. I swallow hard, my eyes jumping up to meet his. He's closed off, eyes dark and brooding, before he opens his mouth to explain.

"Pearling. Silicon beads I had implanted to increase a woman's pleasure…" he says softly. A shudder of filthy desire runs through me at this explanation. How painful must that have been? His commitment to a woman's pleasure makes me feel all warm and tingly. But then, jealousy shoots through me, and I glare, crossing my arms in a pout.

"What woman's?" I growl. He smirks, bending down quickly, trapping my cheeks with the pinch of his deft fingers, gentle enough not to harm me, but hard enough to show his power, his seriousness.

"For your pleasure alone now, dirty fucking slut."

I feel my brows raise in the middle as a whine of wanton need escapes my throat despite how hard I try to stop it. I've spent all my life being the good girl; now, I want to be bad. His eyes blaze over my skin, igniting me again, making my body buzz with excitement. There is no fear of my first time; even if there's pain, I will swallow it whole, allow it to become as much a part of me as they will be in this moment.

His nostrils flare as he pinches my cheeks harder, and knowing how they react when I sink into this new Alice, I can't help but to tease and entice them some more. I stick out my tongue, laying it flat, pushing my face against his hand toward the heavy head of his cock, straining for my first taste as nervous excitement flutters through me.

"Such a bad girl," he hisses, gripping his length with his other hand, bringing his dripping head to my lips. "Open."

He releases my cheeks on his command, and I drop my jaw as wide as it can go. He teases my lips, tracing them with the slick head of his heavy cock as I whine and writhe on the couch beneath him, my own pleasure building knowing that I am making him feel good. He lets go of his cock and smooths his hands over my head, one on each side, cradling my skull as he pulls his hips back slightly, positioning himself at the entrance of my mouth.

"You're going to take it all, baby. Breathe through your nose," he says, slipping into a gentler tone. Our eyes lock, and the trust I need is there; he won't push me beyond what he thinks I am capable of. I obey as he begins to inch his wide, long length into my salivating mouth, his silky head gliding easily along my tongue. My lips close around his cock automatically, and he releases a groan of ecstasy as he shallowly thrusts, allowing me a moment to get used to this new act.

"Look at me when you take my cock in your pretty little mouth, Alice," he growls, and I do. His face is glorious; a fierce archangel sent to pillage and burn and destroy, his long, lean muscles on full display, the bronzed skin of his face flushed with desire. The piercing of his tip rubs against the roof of my mouth, foreign and forbidden and therefore delicious, and the pearls lining his shaft create a pleasurable friction against my tongue. I can only imagine what it will feel like when buried deep in my pussy.

Out of the corner of my eye, I can see Tristan step out of his boxers, his own length springing free, bobbing and surging with desire. He's not pierced or *pearled*, but somehow he's still just as sexy as Jameson. I take a moment to appreciate his thickly muscled thighs, sparse tattoos hiding there as well.

My attention—though it wants to jump everywhere and see everything—is limited, and so I do my best to focus on one thing at a time to savor this. Jameson works his hips, his fingers knotting in my hair, a sneer on his face.

"Suck it, hollow your cheeks."

I take his demand and do just that, suctioning him further into my mouth, rewarded as he hisses through his teeth and pulls out. I am breathing hard, gasping, but he's relentless, and it makes me all the wetter.

"Lick it like a popsicle, little whore."

His words make me whine, and my fingers twitch to grab him, to make it easier, but as soon as I raise my hand, something else is there. Flicking my tongue against his piercing before I run it along his gloriously ribbed and bumped shaft, something heavy and hard and surging settles in my hand. My eyes slip closed as Tristan gives me himself and his own directions.

"Like this, baby," he says with his strained voice, encircling his hand around mine and showing me how to pump his cock just the way he likes. As my fingers wrap around his girth, they don't meet again. Another shiver rips through me as I lick and suck Jameson. He thrusts his hips forward, planting himself deep in my mouth as Tristan releases my hand and lets me stroke him on my own. Jameson's piercing tickles the back of my throat, and tears spring into my eyes as I gag, my jaw aching already from being stretched so wide to accommodate him.

It is in that moment, with a cock in my mouth and one in my hand and my oxygen depleting that I slip into that new Alice, the one whose mind is numb, the one who seeks only to please the two men she's falling hard for, the two men she trusts wholly with her life. This is the Alice that wants the dirtiest things to come to light, the Alice who is finally free of the confines of her mind and societal constraints, the Alice that I lean into with abandon.

Jameson speaks, voice gentle, eyes softening for a moment as he slips out of his dominant mindset.

"When I ease into your throat, baby, breathe through your nose and swallow, try to relax, alright?" he says softly, thumb reaching down to stroke my cheek. Eyes locked on his, I manage a slight nod. "Tap twice on my thigh if it's too much."

The way he's looking at me now, with praise and adoration in his cobalt eyes, makes me even wetter, my thighs slick as they rub helplessly together.

"I wanna see tears running down your face as he fucks your mouth, Alice," Tristan growls as I languidly pump his cock. Before I can even moan, Jameson's feeding me more and more of his rigid length, and I do just as he's instructed. Relax, breathe through your nose. I still gag, and each time he pulls away, allowing a reprieve before he sinks further down my throat. Tears do form in my eyes with each subsequent gag, but I fucking love it. I watch Jameson, how he hisses through his teeth, how he throws his face to the ceiling and curses in Russian.

I continue to suck him, my tongue unable to sit still, rubbing lovingly along his ribbed shaft. His thrusts become more determined, and each time he hits the back of my throat, he holds my head in place, not allowing me the easy way out by pulling away. I pump Tristan's cock faster as I moan and gag.

"I'm…gonna come…" Jameson pants.

"Swallow it all, dirty girl," Tristan commands, and my wide eyes flick to his. His gaze is wild, malicious in a way I've not seen yet as he pulls his cock away from me and instead wipes one of my cheeks free of tears. His gesture warms me.

Jameson pumps one more time, then another, and by the third, he's forced himself as deeply down my throat as he can go, my nose pressing against the flat expanse of muscle above his cock. Tristan grabs my hand quickly, wrapping my own palm around my throat so I can feel the bulge of his length as he shudders and spurts his seed straight down my esophagus.

I go rigid in that second, my head dizzy from lack of oxygen, my clit aching and throbbing to the point where I feel like I can come any second. Before I know what's happened, Jameson pulls out, kneeling down as I rasp in a huge breath, the salty taste of him still potent on my tongue. He presses a lingering kiss on my forehead before he murmurs my reward.

"You did so good taking my cock and cum down your throat, baby girl. I'm so proud of you."

His hands are all over me, reassuring me as I nod and whimper, allowing myself a moment to calm my breathing.

Tristan, however, cannot seem to reign himself in. He swipes the wide, low coffee table clear of remotes and decorative books before he nudges Jameson out of the way. His huge hands engulf my hips, and I manage a dazed smile up at him as he lifts me like a rag doll and lays me on the table.

He hovers over me, his whole body tensed like a coiled spring, his narrow hips between my thighs and his rigid length resting along my hip bone. Part of me knows this is a moment I will never be able to take back, and the cautious side of myself quietly reminds me of that. But as I hold out my hand and Jameson intertwines our fingers, and as Tristan leans down so his elbows are on either side of my head and he gives me his boyish grin, I know that this is the decision I will forever want.

He's slow, his rough, warm hands skimming up my sides as they peel my dress off and toss it away. I'm not wearing a bra since I was too nervous earlier to ask Tristan to find the right one in my drawers. Jameson presses a kiss to my temple as Tristan's hand engulfs one of my breasts, his tongue darting out to flick against my peaked nipple.

I moan on contact, back arching like a bridge over the slab of wood beneath me. So many sensations are erupting around me that I find I'm still in that same headspace—the New Alice one I'm loving so much. Being their slutty little rag doll makes me feel more free in my life than I've ever felt before. I've never taken drugs, but I'm assuming any euphoria-inducing substance would have nothing on this. Part of me wants to try just to prove this hypothesis correct.

"I can't take my time with you, baby," Tristan rasps, his eyes as pale as silver, his chiseled jaw set. I expected this from him; to be unable to control himself when the time actually came. A thrill of fear chases through my veins. I've had their fingers in my pussy, but I know that's vastly different than their cocks. Jameson squeezes my hand, bringing his lips to my ear.

"You'll be alright, *babochka*. You have me here, too. We would never do anything to hurt you."

I turn my gaze to his, ignited and aroused as images of him thrusting into my raw throat flits through my mind's eye. We've reached an entirely new level tonight, and the trust between us feels strong as steel. Pressing his forehead to mine, his lips peck my nose, and I cannot help but give him a watery smile. At the same time, Tristan's thumb is slowly circling my clit with just enough pressure to bring forth an orgasm. I feel it looming as he kisses my cheek before taking my nipple between his teeth and tracing his tongue over the little bud.

I cry out, going rigid with the onslaught of my climax. Just as I'm about to come, Tristan presses his fingers into my pussy, thrusting hard enough that I see stars. It ratchets everything up another notch, and when I finally orgasm, my scream echoes through the house. Without faltering, I feel him withdraw, something else pressing at my entrance—something much, much bigger.

Still shivering from my climax, Jameson captures my lips with his, kissing me slowly and tenderly, trapping my mewls of desire and pain as Tristan eases into me. I can tell he's restraining himself for my benefit, and it warms me.

Jameson pulls away, wiping stray hairs from my eyes, smiling down at me softly.

"Good girl," he croons. My slickness eases the way for Tristan as he finally manages to push the tip of his cock into my no longer virgin pussy. My chest feels like it's on fire, my stomach full of butterflies. "You're doing so well, baby."

I tear my eyes away from Jameson to peer up at Tristan. He's gritting his teeth, hips canting shallowly as he backs out and then proceeds to feed me a few more inches. The stretch and burn is new and painful to a degree, but the further he goes, the less painful it becomes. I don't realize my jaw is slack, my mouth hanging open wide, strange noises exiting my raw throat. One of his hands grips my hip in a possessive hold, the other splayed wide by my head.

It hits me at that moment. I'm having sex for the first time. And it's with my sexy step-brothers who used to frighten me so badly my mother basically banished them. Taking that fear, playing with it, learning how to tame it so that they can hurt and scare anyone else but me—it is the singularly most powerful thing I've ever done or will ever do.

"Fuck, she's so tight," Tristan grunts. "Play with her. Make her come on my cock."

Jameson wordlessly obeys, smoothing his hand down to my pussy to play with my clit while Tristan sinks even deeper into me.

"Look at me, baby," he commands, and I obey. He falls to his elbow, bringing our faces closer before his lips capture mine. He releases my hip, hooking his arm under my right thigh and yanking up, changing the angle and depth of our connection, my knee pressed almost to my ear. In the same moment, he gives a final harsh thrust, his cock spearing me as I cry out against his mouth, his tongue swirling against mine to soothe the sting of becoming his. *Theirs.*

There's something so cathartic about the moment that a sob bubbles up my throat and tears spring into my eyes, pooling before they run down my temples.

Tristan stops moving, brows drawn together in concern, brushing his thumb over my cheek.

"Alice—"

"I'm okay," I say shakily but quickly.

"Then…what—"

"I'm just so happy to…I mean I…I feel…I'm feeling happy for the first time in so long."

My words are a hushed whisper, and everything stills. I wonder if I've scared them, feeling stupid. Like I need to curl up and hide.

But then Tristan grins, and when I turn my gaze, Jameson is smiling softly, too. He says something to me in Russian—something Vasily used to say to my mom that

I recognize but have a feeling he doesn't know I know it. *I love you.* Before I can let those words sink in and fester, he traps my lips in a hard kiss, and Tristan begins to thrust deep within me, short bursts against my womb. He's hitting me somewhere simultaneously painful and pleasurable. Jameson gathers wetness on the pads of his fingers and circles my clit in time with Tristan's thrusts. Through the pain blossoms something beautiful, something I've never felt before.

We're all connected deeply, now. Woven into one another's souls. I'm crying, moaning, whimpering into Jameson's mouth as Tristan begins to pull nearly all the way out before slamming back into me, the slap of our skin and the wet noises my pussy is making spurring me into a new orgasm.

In one hand, I grab Jameson's bicep, and before I can cling to Tristan, he coils his wide palm over my throat, clamping down slowly as my climax builds and builds.

"Faster," he commands Jameson, who obeys, the friction on my clit burning, my stomach knotting as I gasp. My nails dig into Tristan's wrist as he groans, staring down at me with a furious look. I feel the ripples of an orgasm, the first tendrils. Tristan slams into me harder, Jameson's fingers circle me faster. As soon as I gasp, Tristan clamps down, cutting my air supply to half as my orgasm tears through me, shattering me into nothing but shards of beautiful silver glass.

My toes point, my legs so locked that my muscles spasm, my head swims and my entire body feels like it's floating as my pussy clamps his cock again and again and again. I feel my gush of wetness—my squirting, and Tristan pumps into me harder and faster, his hips going rigid before he slams into me so hard blackness dots my vision.

As soon as he lets up, I rasp in a breath, everything

coming back into dizzying focus, my head rushing with another strange wave of euphoria.

"So fucking good for your big brothers, Alice," Tristan pants above me, sweat dotting his smooth chest and face. I can't help but grin lazily, dazed, floating, when Jameson captures my chin, forcing my eyes to his.

His smirk has morphed into his malicious one, and my heart stutters.

"I know you're tired baby, but you're still going to be a good girl and take my cock too, *da*?"

The way he croons the words to me has my body melting, has my cunt clenching and begging to be filled, has me willing to do whatever he commands. So the next words out of my mouth—though a shock to us all—still feel right.

"Yes, daddy," I whimper.

Jameson's nose ticks, his pupils blowing wide, his fingers digging in deep. Tristan pulls out with a rush of our fluids, the slickness coating my thighs and my ass. It's as Jameson and Tristan maneuver me around, bending me over the coffee table with Jameson kneeling between my thighs, that I remember his pierced penis and pearled shaft. A whimper of fear escapes me, and I feel stupid for tempting the devil, but it's too late as he smooths his palms over my ass cheeks, spreading them wide.

He groans at the sight, and I feel his thumb circle and probe at the tight, forbidden entrance. I cry out, lurching away at the new sensation. He yanks my hips back with one hand.

"One day I'll fuck this hole, *babochka*, and Tristan can kiss your tears away when I do. Yes, princess?"

He presses the tip of his thumb just barely inside, just enough to give me a taste of the burn. I whine, gripping the edge of the table. He presses further when I hesitate to answer.

"Yes, yes daddy!" I cry. He pulls his thumb away, and I pant.

"Good girl," he says soothingly, his fingers pushing up into my used cunt, swirling around a mix of all of us. His fingers leave for a moment, and a few seconds later I feel the round edge of his piercing and the thick head of his cock. My body goes slack, but Tristan pulls my hair out of my face, fisting it, rising up on his knees, his cock already erect again. I whine when I understand what he wants, but the thought of how they're using me is so fucking hot.

He slaps my cheek with his heavy cock.

"Open," he growls. I whimper, resisting, pushing him— pushing them both. Jameson is slowly sawing me in half, working his way deeper and deeper. A slap rings out, and a second later, the pain registers on my ass cheek and I cry out.

"Be a good girl, Alice."

I nod, tears gathering at his admonishment, again more cathartic than anything, and I open my mouth wide. Tristan leans down, smoothing his palm over my head.

"You okay, baby girl? You know how much I love you?"

His words make my heart burst, and I nod, crying harder as Jameson sinks fully into me. My sob gurgles off into a moan, and Tristan's tip is pressing against my parted lips, seeking entrance.

"Look at me, baby, I'll make it quick. Going to fuck you raw so every time you swallow tomorrow you think of me."

His sentiments are my cloaked warning, and he slams into my mouth, not stopping until he hits the back of my throat and I choke. Jameson picks up speed but keeps his thrusts deep, making my bare breasts rub across the table. Tristan fists my hair and fucks my mouth. Drool dribbles sloppily down the side of my face as semen and my juices leak out my pussy. Jameson's slick skin slaps against mine,

100

and those pearls? Holy. Fuck.

The piercing is one thing, but to feel that tip rubbing against my deepest parts while also having those big, round pearls stroking along inside me—it's almost too much to bear.

"Go, Tristan, I can't hold on much longer," Jameson pants, fingers digging into my hips. He does just that, slamming down into my throat while his fist encircles my neck, squeezing hard enough that I feel him gripping his cock through me. I can't even feel his climax, but the powerful sneer on his face makes him look like some sort of god in this moment. He slowly withdraws and lets up at the same time as I choke on his seed and rasp in as big of a breath as I can, the taste of myself and him potent on my tongue.

He brushes his fingers through my knotted, sweaty hair, pressing his forehead to mine.

"You're so beautiful when you cry. I see my cum on your lips, fucking gorgeous slut," he hisses with a rueful grin. A pathetic laugh tries to escape my throat, one of sheer ecstasy. But I am soon yanked up and back. A cry leaves my lips as the quick position change deepens the angle at which Jameson is hitting me. I feel him sink onto the leather couch, both of us facing Tristan with me impaled on his lap. He leans back and my exhausted, limp body follows, my skull crashing to his shoulder like so many hours ago in the locker room.

He spreads his legs, and because mine are resting on top, they follow. Tristan, eyeing me like I'm water and he's been in the desert for days, reaches over and pushes against my knees, spreading me even further. At the same time, Jameson grabs my wrists and pins them against the couch cushions. His strokes are slow and deep as we settle into this new position, and my eyes can't help but flit down—only to see his slick, pearled cock slowly withdrawing before disappearing again into me, the roll of his hips so languid.

"Look at what a good girl you are, Alice, taking both our cocks today," Jameson growls in my ear. "Such a perfect slut. I want to watch you squirt all over my cock."

All I can manage is a long whine in response. My body is exhausted, my pussy beginning to feel raw, my throat aching, my eyes slipping closed. At the same time, I love it; I love having no control over my body. I love how they are using me. I love how I know I'll be safe and taken care of forever by them.

Forever.

I think I've known I love them for a while now, but with Tristan on his knees before me, peering into my eyes like I am a goddess, and with Jameson behind me, rocking his strong body against mine, whispering how beautiful I am, it makes it all the more real.

I love them both.

CHAPTER SEVEN

TRISTAN

She's fucking perfect. From the way she cries at the intensity of her emotions during such intimate moments, to the way she smiles lazily up at me with my cum smeared across her lips—she is utter perfection.

Watching Jameson fuck other women can be hot, and no, not because I am attracted to my twin fucking brother. It is hot watching the action itself, watching the woman obtain pleasure, seeing how you yourself would look while fucking. So watching Jameson—the only person left in this world I trust wholeheartedly—fuck Alice slowly as she lolls and whimpers in his lap?

My aching cock pitifully surges in an attempt to rise again so quickly. I know by the end of the night I'll have drained myself completely.

My eyes feast on her spread pussy being speared by such a thick cock, my semen and her juices easing his way. My fingers dig more deeply into the soft flesh around her knees. Images of her swirly handwriting festers in my mind's eye. The thing she wants to do the most. The thing that may hurt her—something we've never done but already decided we'd be willing to try if she really did want it.

She wants us both in her cunt at the same time.

I don't have much time to fantasize about her fantasy when Jameson rasps out, "Suck her clit. Make her come all over my cock."

I don't even hesitate, even when Alice comes alive at his demand and whimpers and pleads that she can't go again.

"Shh, baby. I know," I coo gently.

I grin at her swollen little nub before I suck it between my lips, swirling my tongue around it. She gasps and her hips jerk, all while Jameson pumps slowly but forcefully into her tight cunt. It's a dance, a type of tango to try and stay out of his way, to not interrupt his pleasure. It is just as much of a tango to try and ensure I am focusing on her, listening to her responses, watching the way her svelte body shivers and reacts to our touches.

"No, no, no," she cries, trying to close her legs. I keep them open, digging my fingers further into her thighs, eyes flitting up to her face to ensure she's okay. Her head is thrown back onto Jameson's shoulder, the tendons in her neck tight as ropes, her brows pinched together and her mouth open on another silent plea. The way her little white teeth dance over her lip, wanting to bite it but unable to quell her own moans, has me fucking rock hard again.

Jameson's hold on her wrists is just as tight as my hold on her thighs. He increases the speed of his thrusts slightly, and she thrashes her head.

"Please, please," she begs, choking off in a cry as he thrusts even harder and my tongue flicks faster. Jameson answers in a growl.

"Take my cock deep in your pussy like a good girl, Alice. I want to feel you get tight around me."

More whimpers, her thighs restless. Her perky little tits bounce as Jameson begins to fuck her, driving up into her hard and fast but still utterly rhythmic and controlled. I don't understand how he has such restraint.

"Come on daddy's cock, baby."

"I-I can't," she sobs. A sharp slap rings out, and Alice lurches as I grin against her wet, hot pussy. Jameson's handprint blooms on the inside of her thigh. She's so red and swollen, I do feel a sting of pity. But she has a safe word, and she hasn't chosen to use it.

"Oh, I think she likes being punished," Jameson hisses. He's right; just after the crack of skin on skin, she'd gone rigid and breathless, tightening up like a coiled spring. I suck against her clit with wet, sloppy noises as Jameson pistons in and out of her faster and faster. I push her over the edge as I graze my teeth teasingly over her bundle of nerves. She rewards us both as she spasms, clenching and unclenching before she releases a garbled scream.

I slow my licks as she spasms, Jameson's cock now coated in her juices.

"Fuck...me..." he growls as I pull away from a limp Alice. He tenses and climaxes—fucking hard. I can see it in the way his body pulses in time with each shot of his seed deep inside her. With a hiss, he gives a few more pumps, Alice whining, lolling like a used rag doll against him. His cum leaks out of her pussy and onto his softening cock.

He leaves himself planted deep inside her; he's told me to try this before, but I'm too impatient. Why just warm your cock when you can fuck?

Everything in the living room seems to be perfectly still, like time and space and the world is on pause. This is the quietest my brain has been in a long ass time. Staring up at Alice's slack form as Jameson's eyes flick open to storm down at me is such an intense, charged moment, but it is tempered by the peace that surrounds us all.

As wrong as this feels, it feels just as right.

And if something like this can give my fucked up brain peace? Then so be it.

JAMESON

Alice is limp in my arms with my soft cock still cradled in her poor, used pussy. I'm not sure what she's thinking, which is concerning, but I am simply following her lead. Whatever she wants is up to her, and we will comply.

Tristan has a far away dreamy look on his face, but his eyes roam over Alice's flesh with a look of such adoration it makes my dead heart swell just a little. He's never been in love—but I can see it here and now. He's truly in love with her, just as deeply as I am. She's so fucking perfect for us.

Which is why I am beginning to become nervous the longer she doesn't move.

I give in slowly, wrapping my arms around her, nuzzling my cheek against her head. Tristan releases her knees, smoothing his palms up her soft thighs in a show of comfort.

"Are you alright, *babochka*?" I ask gently.

"Mmm, yes," she responds, sounding exhausted. There's a different note to her voice, though—higher pitched. As though she might—

Her body tenses, but she can't hold it in. She bursts into a sob that cuts so deeply into my chest I feel faint. Tristan and I both move at the same time, cautiously but efficiently. I pull out as he jumps up to grab towels. I maneuver Alice around like a bride, folding her in on herself as she shakes. My mind is racing. Fuck, how bad did we fuck up? We were open and honest and she agreed. We checked in with her during. What could we have missed?

Tristan is back, a few dry towels and one warm wet rag. His brows are pinched, his eyes full of the same concern swirling in my mind. Before we can ask, she speaks.

"I-I'm sorry. I'm-I'm okay. J-just emotional."

That eases some tension. Tristan sits at the end of the couch, quietly waiting as she calms down. I glance at him over the top of her head and whisper in Russian to him.

"Sub-drop."

He frowns and nods, his eyes flicking to her, giant hands clasped around the bundle of towels as they dangle between his spread knees. I bite back a snort as Alice sniffles into my chest and I slowly rub my hand up her arm. She won't understand how to process this aspect of the sex we enjoy, the sex she fantasizes about; after sustaining adrenaline for such a lengthy period of time, that drop can trigger a ton of shit. Insecurities, self-doubts, fear of rejection or abandonment.

Tristan gets up, and I can hear him rummaging around for a glass before the water spout in the fridge kicks on.

109

Reaching for the wet rag, I bring it around, pressing a soft kiss to Alice's sweaty temple.

"You did so good, baby, taking our cocks, coming so hard for us."

She whines against me. I bring the rag to her knee, letting her adjust to the warmth before I slip it up her leg.

"I'm so proud of you, beautiful girl. Let me clean you up. Then you need some water, *da*?"

"Yes," she whispers against me. Tenderly as I can, I swipe the rag between her legs. She bucks with a whine, curling her face into my neck.

"I know, baby. You're so brave. Did so well," I murmur in encouragement, my lips hovering over her forehead as I cleanse her. Tristan returns, kneeling in front of us with a glass of water and a bowl of grapes. She'll need the hydration and the natural sugars to help her even out. I nudge her head with my chin.

"Look at Tristan. I'll explain what you're feeling."

She obeys, turning to him almost greedily, lurching toward him like he's the sun. I know the only reason she stops is because she also wants me. She needs us close. The reassurance, then. I breathe another small sigh of relief.

Tristan holds the water to her lips, and she guzzles it.

"Tell me how you feel, physically. And if you're not ready to talk, that's okay, too," I assure her calmly. She's drained the entire glass. A slight blush coats her cheeks, her eyes a little brighter. Rubbing her plump, swollen lips together, she considers the question. Her cheeks redden more.

"Umm...sore...down there. And really, really tired."

I brush a few strands of hair from her eyes.

"All normal. You're staying home tomorrow, and the day after, if you need to. The pain will go away with time and rest."

"And it won't always hurt like that after," Tristan adds gently. She turns her gaze to his, and I watch as he fights back a huge grin.

"It's just...new," she murmurs, shifting her hips against me before she winces. Tristan chuckles.

"What about emotionally?"

Tristan's smile slowly melts off his face like candle wax at my question. Alice turns her face back up, but she looks instead at the ceiling. Her brows slowly inch closer and closer together, her eyes betraying how tired she is, rimmed in red from her crying.

"It's...the happiest I've been in so long. I think...I think I cried because I actually felt something other than just anxiety or sadness," she whispers, almost lulled into a trancelike state. I give her a moment before I press on that note a little more, peeling back the layers of her psyche.

"What else did you feel besides fear?"

"Joy," she says quickly. "Attachment. Safety. But...I think what made all those emotions stronger were the opposites of them. I...I was terrified. Questioned my morals, questioned whether or not you'd...hurt me," she says softly. Tristan bristles.

"We'd never—"

"Her feelings are valid, brother. It takes a shit-ton of trust to do what we did."

He tucks tail at my slight admonishment, but Alice presses on.

"I don't understand why...why I want to just have you lay on me...lay close to me...praise me more..." she mumbles the last part. I understand her aura quickly, so to speak. How she desires to be handled without question or hesitation after such intensity. Shifting around, I lay down, pulling her on top of me, but keeping her between my legs and lower down, so her head rests just under my ribs. I throw the blanket over her shoulders while Tristan maneuvers between her legs and rests his chest on her ass.

We're both touching her intimately, using our bodies as shields against the outside world. She's shivering against us, but it quickly calms. I stroke my fingers through her long, thick hair while Tristan gently rubs circles in her shoulders. Every so often, a small whimper will escape her throat, and she'll sniffle like she wants to cry again, at which point we do as she's told us she wants: we praise her.

"You're safe, *babochka*," Tristan rumbles, bringing one hand down to grip a palmful of her ass.

"You're fucking beautiful, my strong girl. You took my thick cock down your throat so well."

It continues like this for an indeterminable amount of time. Alice relaxes piece by piece, melting into us in a sort of lucid state. My cock is nestled between her breasts. I can feel every beat of her heart, every breath she takes. I'm half-hard already. I can tell by the way Tristan is shifting around that he is, too.

I suppose she'll have to build her stamina.

My eyes lock with Tristan's after a while, and I quirk my brow at him. A devious smirk paints his face. This is, after all, nothing Alice hasn't explicitly said she's wanted. Tristan begins to rub himself into a full erection, gently prying her legs apart. She tenses, waking up a little, raising her head to try and look back at what Tristan is doing. I capture her cheeks with my hands, forcing her eyes to mine.

Her big blue eyes are so full of fear. She's terrorized, her heart hammering in her chest so hard it feels like it's rubbing against my cock. Tristan drips a wad of spit onto his dick, his fingers spreading her thighs further, his knees moving up to keep her spread. She's whimpering, her fearful eyes locked on mine, her bottom lip wobbling, tears brimming, held back by the dam of her eyelashes. I stroke my thumbs across her apple tinted cheeks as Tristan works his fingers into her from behind.

"You can say it, *babochka*. But we know you want this," I whisper tenderly to her. Lip trembling more fiercely, her tears slip loose and cascade down her cheeks. Tristan plants his palm across her lower back, sinking her into the cushions as he rubs his tip at her swollen entrance.

She chokes on a whimper, her pupils pinpointed in her fear. The sight makes my cock ache, my heart race, my lip curl back viciously as my fingers dig into her cheek bones.

Before I fully devolve into my dominant side, I ask her again.

"Do you need to quit, baby girl? It's okay if you do."

I can tell by the way her jaw drops that he's worked his head into her tight cunt. He raises his knee, bringing it outside her thighs so that he can clamp her legs together around his length, giving me the perfect view of the rounded hills of her ass as he fucks her from behind, all the while making her tits grind on my cock.

After a moment, she shakes her head.

"Take me. *Use* me."

"Fuck," I hiss, pushing my fingers through her hair. In her diary, she wrote about being taken while she was asleep. It's actually quite a common kink, one I've always wanted to indulge in but never found the right partner to do it with. And with Alice willing, compliant, and so close all the time, I have a feeling this will become one of my favorite acts.

It calls to me as a dominant. Seeing her fear and her tears arouses me, but not for sinister reasons. It arouses me because I know she'll let me and Tristan ravage her. She wants us to when she's in the right head space. This type of intimacy calls to her as a submissive; by being able to enter into an uncontrollable, fearful type of play, she's able to make the experience her own. She is able to be afraid and feel safe at the same time, which will empower her—because if someone truly attacked her, there would be no choice, no trust or safety.

Being able to dominate her while simultaneously empowering her is the sexiest goddam thing on this planet. I begin to rock my hips, sliding my cock between her tits, my fingers knotted deeply in her hair. Tristan still has one palm splayed over her lower back, the other gripping her hip. He bites his lip as he begins to rock into her with hard, deep strokes, the slap of his skin on her ass making me remember what it was like to be buried in her sweet pussy.

"Keep your eyes on me. You don't have to come this time, baby, but you still will."

She shakes her head the best she can as I fuck her tits and Tristan rams into her beautiful little pussy. Her neck bows, unable to support the weight of her head with how exhausted she is. I release her hair to grip her chin, forcing her face up. Her eyes are slitted, fluttering, her mouth a perfect 'o' just waiting to be filled.

Tristan slaps her ass, and she yelps, eyes widening at the same time I slip my two middle fingers into her petite mouth, resting them on her tongue, just barely grazing the back of her throat. Her tongue fights me as she gags, raising her ass in an attempt to get away. Tristan spanks her again, cursing her out in Russian. I smirk at her helplessness, her eyes watering as I give her a small reprieve.

"You like this, don't you, filthy girl?" I sneer. "I'm going to come all over your tits and chin, and you're going to lick it off me, understand?"

Before she can nod, I press my fingers to the back of her throat again, and tears leak down her cheeks as she gags. I lean in, softening my voice.

"You can tap me twice if you're done, Alice."

Her eyes glint like steel for a moment before they go

back to terrified. Satisfied with her consent, I roll my hips faster against her. Tristan drops another wad of spit between her ass cheeks, and I grin ruefully, knowing what she's in for. If she's going to take us both at the same time, she needs to start practicing now.

"Suck my fingers like you're gonna suck my cock tomorrow, slut."

Whining, she obeys before a garbled scream vibrates my hand, Tristan's thumb popping past the tight band of her asshole. She claws her way up my torso, impaling her throat on my fingers as Tristan simply follows, trapping her even tighter. My cock has lost its plush home between her breasts, but her stomach is just as soft, wet with our sweat and my pre-cum.

She falters, collapsing on my chest. I thread my fingers through her hair at the back of her scalp, turning her face to the side and keeping my fingers planted deep in her mouth. Tristan grunts, pulls his thumb out, spits into her fluttering hole, and presses his middle finger into her virgin ass. She sobs and chokes, nails digging into my sides, but she doesn't tap out.

I give her head a shake.

"I said suck my fingers, whore."

She begins to suck them like a pacifier.

"God, you're such a good fucking girl," I whisper, encouraging her when it feels she may need it. At my praise, I feel her relax a fraction.

"Get ready to come," Tristan growls to me. I thrust my hips quicker. It won't take much, and I know what it is he wants me to do. She'll have to lick up my cum another time. He slams into her so hard she bites down on my fingers with a scream. He holds her hips and plants his cock as deeply inside her as he can, a victorious sneer on his face as he marks her again.

Alice goes slack, breathing harshly around my fingers, drooling onto my chest. Panting, Tristan takes a moment before he pulls out. As soon as he's free and standing, I flip Alice onto her back, ruck her legs up with my arms, pushing her knees almost to her ears, and slam my cock into her.

She blubbers, cheeks and eyes puffy. But her hands stray up from her sides, palms cupping her breasts, fingers tweaking her nipples.

"Fuck, such a naughty slut," I hiss. "Are you gonna squirt all over my cock again, little whore?"

She whines, pinching her nipples harder, arching her back.

"I bet you love having all this cum in your pussy. You want it leaking out of you for days, don't you?"

One of her hands bravely darts down, tiny fingers circling her clit.

"Bad girl. You like being forced too, don't you? You like it when you're asleep and we stick our cocks in you."

Her pussy flutters around my cock at my words. I groan again. Fuck, she is the hottest being to ever have walked this god-forsaken earth.

"Go on, little slut. Enjoy making yourself come on my cock. This is the only time I'll ever let you touch yourself."

Her neck makes a bridge on the couch as the leather squeaks with each slapping thrust. Mouth dropping wide, she gasps, and then her walls clamp down on me so hard it verges on painful. As soon as I feel her rush of fluids, I can't help but to shoot my load deep into her pussy.

I drop onto her, leaving my cock buried in her, trapping her delicate face with my hands. I shower her with kisses as she sighs and cries softly at the intensity of this moment.

"Such a good girl," I whisper as she falls asleep beneath me.

CHAPTER EIGHT

TRISTAN

A few blissful weeks fly by. It consists of a learning curve for all of us, but we seem to have settled into our roles more seamlessly than any of us thought we would. It is no small thing to watch as Alice blossoms into herself; she smiles all the time, her cheeks always risen, her eyes crinkled from sheer happiness. Jameson watches her like a fucking hawk, but in his eyes I see a softness that only she can coax out of him. She's learning to lean on us when she needs to, and unlearning certain traits that contributed to her depression.

She even got the role of Anne Wheeler in her school's

play. Jameson already ensured we'd have every night off so we could see each performance. We sat outside the school while she took her SATs, we helped stamp her college admission letters, and we make sure we're at every volleyball game, even if I've almost been kicked out twice for harassing the referees.

I throw the dish towel over my shoulder, leaning my hip against the counter as I feast upon her demure, whimsical beauty. She sits perched on a barstool, cheek in her fist, eyes narrowed at her physics homework. Jameson is seated next to her, tapping the eraser to the countertop as he tries to solve the problem. She peeks at him, a slight blush creeping into her cheeks, but I can tell it isn't a lustful glance; it's a nervous one.

She struggles with math, and struggles even more with asking for help. I am beginning to realize why that may be.

"Wasn't this hard when we were in school," Jameson mutters, annoyed with himself. I snort, turning back around to check on the lasagna in the oven. Alice spent most of her afternoon helping me prep it—which ended up with both of us covered in an array of ingredients and a subsequent shower-fuck. I think Jameson is still jealous, but I'll give him his time with her tonight. It's all about balance.

When I turn back around, Alice is shredding the cuticles around her thumbs. I reach across the counter, dropping my hand over hers to still her anxious habit. She jumps at the contact, sitting straighter, coming out of her muddled thoughts. When her bright blue eyes reach mine, they calm, and she gives me a small smile.

"No need to be nervous, *babochka*. Big bro won't let your grades slip," I say with a wink. She peeks at him and chews her lip, a wavering smile on her flawless face. My twin drops his pencil, turning his torso to instead scrutinize her.

"Why are you so nervous, Alice?" he asks. She's quick to shake her head and attempt to play it off, but we catch one another's eye with a knowing look; she is worried about something, but she's not telling us. I release her hand as Jameson turns to face her, spreading his knees and gripping her chair so she has no choice but to look right at him. Her golden blonde hair swishes across her slender shoulders, catching the pale autumn light of October.

He quirks a brow. "Have we done something to make you nervous?" he presses. I let him lead on these instances. He's more keen, more able to pinpoint the thoughts she does not wish to share. I've found I am more her comfort, the one who can make her laugh even when she doesn't want to.

"No, no I promise," she says softly, shaking her head again. "I just seriously suck at math and…asking for help…"

"Who used to help you?"

Fuck, he's good. I lean back against the opposite counter, watching him interrogate her gently. No wonder father honed those skills for him, while he turned me into a monster who could feel no pain and had a stomach of steel to match. I pray every day Alice will never understand the brutality that surrounds our lives; she is astute, and we know she knows something, but the less she knows right now, the better.

Her small, pained voice snaps my attention back to her, my fists clenching and knuckles popping.

"My…dad…"

Jameson's eyes flash to me in warning. The urge to smash something—preferably that piece of shit's skull—overcomes me.

He shifts, reaching out and gathering her hands into his. Before he can speak, I beat him to it.

"We're not him, Alice. We won't yell or think you're stupid."

121

Her eyes flick to mine, and in their depths I can see she's relaxed a fraction. After holding my gaze, she pinches her face and shakes her head.

"I know that. I do. It's just—"

"It will take time," Jameson says soothingly, though I can hear the restraint in his voice. He wants to kill that fucker as much as I do. She gave us permission to seek the files on that night—the night her father was taken to jail. Her social worker seemed glad to give them over to us, even sliding in a card for a therapist who specializes in childhood trauma of that magnitude.

I know of one sure way to stem my own feelings of fury, but Jameson is right; it will take time. Planning. I can't kill that piece of scum without his help, anyways. Reading the file was much like reading her diary; like peering through a looking glass to a specific thought in her beautiful mind. Only, this time it had been a nightmare.

She'd been concussed, bruised, vessels in her bright blue eyes burst, her teeth—not yet adult, thankfully— knocked out. And for everything our *babochka* had endured that night, her blessed mother had endured it ten-fold in a sacrificial act to save her daughter.

Her biological father is living on borrowed time.

She takes a shuddering breath, eyes glossed as she stares at Jameson's chest and nods.

"I know," she says softly, though her voice cracks. My heart cracks along with it. Jameson's temples flare as he grits his teeth, his eyes boring into hers with passionate intensity. We know we love her already; we suspect she may love us as well, but we know we must wait until she comes to that conclusion on her own. We will in no way sway her decision.

Jameson moves, scooting her homework sheets together and filing them back into her binder. There's a smile on his face, but it doesn't fucking fool me.

"Let me look over this tonight and figure it out so I don't have to sit here and feel an idiot, *da*?" he teases, voice gravelly. Her shoulders drop and her smile is now genuine.

"Thank you," she says softly before she bites her lip again and reddens to a tomato. I quirk my brow at her with a smirk, waiting for whatever else she seeks to say. "Umm…I also…kinda have a big question…and you can totally say no, but I've never done it before and I really want to and—"

I've rounded the counter, wrapping her in a bear hug from behind as I bury my face in her silky hair, inhaling her scent. "Spit it out, baby, before I throw your adorable ass on this counter and make you moan."

Jameson snorts at the same time she gasps, swatting at me.

"Just…I was wondering if I could have a birthday party here. Well, like a birthday-slash-Halloween party since it's so close…."

My eyes find my twin's over her shoulder. I can see his hesitation, but I silently plead with him on this; she's never had a *real* birthday party? Like the ones we used to sneak out to? His eyes never leave mine, but his face softens from granite to shale. And then, his lips curl up like that damn Cheshire cat Alice loves so much.

"On one condition, *babochka*."

My smirk rivals his as I bring my lips to her ear, eyes on him.

"You let us join the festivities," I say. She stiffens in my arms.

"But…"

Her voice is worried. We've had to discuss this aspect of our relationship; no one can know, not even her friends. As soon as she's graduated, we're more in the clear, and depending on where she chooses to go to college, we've already discussed moving with her. This world still looks down its nose at relationships that stray from the status quo, but we don't fucking care. She's ours, and someday, *everyone* will know.

The door to Alice's room is cracked slightly, soft light spilling into the desolate hallway. She's done well communicating when she needs space, when she needs time to think or be a normal almost-eighteen year old, but I still pace in front of her room. Every time I catch a glimpse of golden blonde hair spilling over her bare shoulders, her lip pinched between her teeth as she writes furiously into her diary, my dick gets that much harder.

Distracted, my boot knocks into a decorative table, and Alice snorts softly.

"You're too big to be sneaky, Tristan. I've been seeing your shadow for fifteen minutes."

Grinning to myself, I push her door open with my toe, leaning against the door jamb and crossing my arms, leveling her with a smirk. She's wearing a tank top and itty bitty sleep shorts, knowing full-well that when she struts around in them our restraint typically snaps and we end up making her scream our names like a violent prayer.

"Wasn't too long ago I sat right there and read your diary. Should've seen how much cum—"

"Tristan!" she hisses, blushing furiously but still giggling. I toss her a wicked smirk. Her room—in the weeks we've been intimate—has started showing more and more signs of life, of who she is. Pictures of her and her friends are tacked to a cork board. Her bookshelf is overflowing with psychology texts—her desired major that she's already studying for. A wildflower scented candle flickers near the window where a vase of dried flowers still sit perched in their vase; flowers we bought for her to congratulate her on snagging her role in that play. Seeing her come to life has breathed life back into me.

Before her, we were empty vessels spawned for the sole purpose to maim and kill. We are the Stefanovs, the right hand men of the Volkov empire. We've seen and done things that would put Jack the Ripper to shame. Yet as soon as we're home with Alice, all that fades away; she is our light in the darkness, our beacon, our lighthouse in a raging sea.

And us? We're still darkness, but now we're *her* darkness; she can use us in whichever way pleases her or brings her joy or catharsis. And judging by the blush still tainting her cheeks, whatever she was just writing is probably going to be just as dark as I like it.

As soon as her round blue eyes find mine again, I'm already stepping into her room, fingers popping the button of my jeans, boots thudding like a war drum as the pulse in her neck ticks harder. Her body subtly shifts, going languid, and I know without either of us saying a thing that she's slipping into her favorite headspace, the one where she's told us she doesn't have to think; she just has to feel and please and be pleased. A violent shudder tears through my body at the sight and what it does to me. Slipping my hand into my jeans, I fist my throbbing cock with a malicious smirk.

"Open wide, little girl."

ALICE

"Fuck, it's way colder than I thought it'd be," Josie complains, bouncing in line next to me. I can't help but grin from ear to ear, the frosty air biting my cheeks as the watery sun dips behind the mountains. It is freezing, our breath puffing out in foggy clouds, but I've never felt more warm, more alive.

Jameson and Tristan agreed to let me have a party. Like, a *real* bash, the kind I used to get invited to but never went because I wanted to make sure Aunt Mary was doing alright. After arguing, Jameson rolled his eyes and let Tristan buy us booze, saying we were going to be drinking whether he provided it or not. As long as we stay at the house, we're good. And knowing Josie has Molly…this night is going to be one for the books.

I feel slightly guilty for not telling them that I plan to dabble in illicit drugs, but I feel like they'll be understanding. They promised to keep their distance tonight at the party and let us all do our thing, but the haunted maze?

"Jesus, Ellie, if you look over your shoulder again you're going to snap your neck from your shoulders," Josie teases. Distracted, my eyes flash to Ellie, who's standing slightly behind us, biting her lip until blood rushes to the surface. Frowning, I tilt my head to the side and study her.

She's been so closed-off lately, so jumpy and depressed. The other day she asked me about getting on birth control, and I'd wondered if she maybe had a secret boyfriend she wasn't ready to share with us yet. If anyone understands that, I totally do, but I'm still worried for my friend.

Reaching out, I rub her puffy jacket where her arm is hiding. She gives us both an unconvincing smile. There are bags under her eyes, and her hair is swept into a ponytail, lacking its usual luster. Ever since that dinner…she's changed.

"Just…the thought of wandering through a corn maze with guys in masks wielding chainsaws…isn't this how all horror movies start? A group of girls go to have fun and then get chopped into little bitty pieces?"

"Wow, okay, that took a morbid turn," Josie teases. We all laugh, but in Ellie's whiskey-hued eyes, there's something raw and real and truly frightened, as though this thought has occurred to her more than once.

"Trust me, girl, we'll be safe," I say, to which she smiles and rolls her eyes, shaking her thoughts loose.

"I know, I know," she sighs, a dense fog creeping in as the last of the sunlight slinks away between the mountains. The scent of fried pumpkin donuts and buttery popcorn permeates the air. Josie clutches a steaming cup of fragrant cider as crunchy orange and yellow leaves tumble by. After a few more minutes of bouncing in line, waiting for our turn while chainsaws and screams light up the night, we finally move up a few spots.

A blissful groan nearly escapes my lips with the movement.

The only reason I know we're completely safe from freaks tonight is because there are two devils hiding somewhere nearby, always watching, always hungry for me. I have no idea what they have planned, but they promised me tonight

I'd be receiving some form of a birthday present.

Currently, one is residing in my pussy, my juices leaking out around the vibrator that settles with a slight heaviness inside me, the other half jutting out to rest over my clit. Apparently, they can operate it from their phones. And as I shift in line again, making that slick silicon slide against my engorged clit, I nearly lose my breath as I choke on a moan.

They say this maze takes three hours to complete.

This is going to be the sweetest torture I think I've ever endured.

It's almost pitch black as we trudge over uneven ground, the chill now soaking into our bones. Josie's teeth are chattering, and in her long braids pieces of corn husk stick out. At one point, a masked chainsaw wielder had popped out, and she'd dived straight for the corn. We're laughing now, but at the moment it had taken us by surprise, and Ellie had booked it without waiting for us.

Every so often, the blue of her phone lights up her face as she checks it for something, but she's quick to shove it back into her North Face jacket. The moon is absent tonight because of the dense fog, and everything has a sheen of dew on it. But between my legs? A fucking waterfall has been turned on, and there's no way it's about to stop anytime soon.

Just as we round another corner, filled to the brim with apprehension, the vibrator thrums to life on its lowest setting, my pussy clenching around it and begging for a release that I've been teased with for over an hour. Breath whooshes from my lungs as I attempt to keep the sharp moan behind my teeth, but as I pause to adjust my hips, restraining from humping the air like a bitch in heat, Josie turns around and quirks her brow at me.

"You good?"

"Just my…shoes…blisters," I breathe, swiping my hair from my sticky forehead. The vibrator clicks off, and I bite my tongue to keep from screaming in frustration. My cunt pulses and clenches, begging for a release that feels so close before it's cruelly ripped away.

Ellie's wide eyes search the darkness between corn stalks.

"Let's keep moving," she whispers, biting her lip again. I understand her fear; this is fucking creepy, and knowing a jump scare could be around any corner is actually quite thrilling for me. The fear of this night, coupled with my insane heightened arousal, has turned me into an entirely new Alice, one that wants to find the nearest masked chainsaw wielding villain and beg him to bend me over and fuck me so hard I see stars.

Shit, I've even considered sneaking off into the corn to finish myself before I explode. But I just nod, unable to trust my voice, and we start forward again. Ellie and Josie are side by side now with a considerable gap between us, but if they keep ignoring me and I keep moving just… like…*that*…

On the precipice of that tidal wave, a chainsaw whirs to life. Ellie screams, tugging Josie forward in a mad sprint, and the fear and the adrenaline and the arousal coursing through me makes me scream as well—but for an entirely different reason. The vibrator chooses that moment to flare to life on its highest setting, and the climax that tears through me has me saying things no good girl should say as my thighs quiver and my breath leaves me in ragged puffs.

Whimpering as I come down from the high, I feel almost like I wet my pants, but I know better, now. Thankfully, the actor chose to chase the two screaming banshees, leaving me blissfully alone to ride out one of the most intense orgasms of my life. Smiling and unaware in that ecstasy, I start forward again before I realize I'm truly alone.

Fuck.

Gulping, I take stock of what I see; corn, a darkened path before me and behind me, and up ahead a fork in the maze. Shit. Which way would they have gone? More distant screams pierce the night as I step forward on trembling legs, still floating from the intensity of that climax.

A half-hour goes by in which I see no one and hear nothing. Josie left her phone in the car, and Ellie hasn't answered hers. My skin prickles in the blackness of the night. I begin to wonder if I've traipsed out of the range of *their* phones as well, since the vibrator has remained off inside me; the heaviness was torture after that mind-numbing euphoria and subsequent tightening of my lower stomach, but now that the sensitivity is residing, it's beginning to feel really fucking good again.

A wicked grin curls on my face. Maybe I'll just go pleasure myself since no one is around. Just as I'm about to step off the path and into the corn, a twig snaps, the sound reverberating in the stillness of the night. Something, an invisible hand of premonition, tightens its fist around my neck. Something lingers and pricks at the back of my mind like a thorn. Ellie's fear…her checking her phone every five seconds in line, her wanting to go on brith control for no apparent reason, her unrealistic fear of a cheesy haunted corn maze…is someone…after her?

And if so, would they settle for me right now since I'm all alone?

Fear clutching at my chest, I pause my strides and take in my surroundings. Jameson and Tristan are here; they're in the parking lot, last I checked. I know if I needed them, they'd find me fast. But would it be fast enough?

Another twig snaps behind me, and I whirl, heart leaping into my throat as the wavering dark figure of a man stands behind me, blocking the path. Lip trembling, I take one step back, fear igniting my veins into something fiery and uncontrollable. The figure is wearing black from head to toe, even his face covered in some type of mask. *Holy shit.* This is happening. The actors are all supposed to be dressed like rednecks or zombies, not like lethal cat burglars.

The figure takes one step closer, bringing his mask into sharp clarity. The lower half is studded with spikes, and over the portion covering his eyes are X's. His hood is drawn up, his shoulders broad, his height insurmountable. Fuck fuck fuck.

Fingers fumbling with my jacket pocket, tears springing into my eyes, I attempt to grab my phone to call my step-brothers—the men I love, the men I trust, the men who will keep me safe. Before I can move, the figure shakes his head slowly, and all the blood drains from my body as a long serrated knife flashes near his thigh from his gloved hand.

The whimper that leaves me is high, frightened, and a steady pulse beats in my cunt, traitor she is. But something stems some of that fear, and it's when the figure finally speaks.

"Run, little *babochka.* Let's see how far you can make it."

Eyes flying wide, I take Jameson at his threat with a cry, turning to flee through the night from two of the most lethal hunters on this planet.

I don't make it far. Stumbling over rocks and dried cobs of corn has me moving much slower. In the very back of my mind, I know I am safe, but the fear thrumming through my veins is just as potent as if I were really being chased by a predator who wants to ravage me in the worst of ways. Something about Jameson right now is different, and part of me seems to know that he's allowing me a glimpse of the man he truly is, the man Tristan also is; men their father made them into.

I only ever saw Vasily really pissed off one time, and he'd made my mother and I leave the house while he dealt with what he called an *employee*. That memory pushes to the forefront of my mind, and everything begins to sink into place. They are dangerous, evil men—but they are also *my* evil, dangerous men, and there is a sort of power born out of the fear of such darkness.

He catches me all too quickly, and I suck in a breath to scream into the night, but he claps his hand over my mouth and drags me between the stalks and further into the blackest parts of the night. Whimpering and kicking and struggling, his hard-muscled body is given a true chance to subdue me—only it's pitiful how weak I am compared to him. A dark chuckle sounds from somewhere and nowhere all at once, and I know Tristan is watching, salivating, a savage hunter with his sights set on his favorite prey.

"Keep struggling, *babochka*. I'll make sure to fuck the fight right out of you."

His words send fire into my veins. I fight all the harder, his leather gloved hand smooth and supple across my lips, and—surprisingly—tears start to prick my eyes. Ones of true fear, ones of the pain of relinquishing my control and surrendering to a more powerful being. I know why I am crying, and it has nothing to do with our relationship. It all has to do with a release that is long overdue; a rewrite of the worst night of my life, wondering if I would live to see another day, wondering if the man that made me would be the man that killed me *and* my mother.

"Fuck, I love hearing her sobs."

Tristan's voice wavers from all around us, deep and menacing. They've slipped into who they are outside of this relationship, and a thrill chases through me. They're being just as vulnerable right now as I am, and it makes my heart ache for the dichotomy they bring to life.

We're in a small clearing, that much I can tell. Jameson holds me from behind, pinning my arms to my sides, my feet flailing in an attempt to fight off whoever chooses to come for me first. My breathing is sharp, the air in my lungs crisp, and everything is heightened; my vision sharpens, my hearing is pinpointed, and every brush of fabric against me ignites my soul. The vibrator still in me now feels like an unwanted intrusion; I need it out of me, and as my fear begins to crest, Tristan materializes in front of me.

His mask is familiar, a rendition of Venom; grinning sleek black skull with rows upon rows of deadly teeth, tongue wickedly lolling, eyes slanted and depthless and somehow bright. I feel Jameson's mask at my ear, his fingers tightening over my mouth.

"Safe word?"

The second his hand slips away, I whisper it. "*Sherbet*."

"Promise, Alice?"

"Yes, *daddy*," I say, jutting my hips back to dig my ass

133

against his raging hard cock. Tristan chuckles, the sound so deep and menacing, sending shivers erupting over my body. Jameson nuzzles my temple, and I wallow in the sweetness for a moment, knowing it's all I will receive until this is over.

"Make yourself useful and tie her up," Jameson hisses, throwing me to his twin. Tristan catches me even as I try to dodge them and make a run for it, my heart in my throat. It doesn't take him long to wrangle my wrists behind my back and slip zip ties around them.

"You'll never escape us, baby. Be good or it'll hurt worse," he seethes, gripping my hair and yanking my head to the side. It forces me to stare up into the dead eyes of his mask, and while I'm drowning in my stark fear and insane arousal, Jameson reaches around my hips from behind, fingers curling into the waistband of my leggings before a gloved hand disappears into my panties. His fingers skim over my wetness, and—gently—he pulls the vibrator from within me, my pussy clenching and struggling to hold it in.

Whimpers leave my lips in puffs. When his hand is free, he casts the toy carelessly aside, and the rumble in both their chests alert me to something they're seeing. My eyes home in on Jameson's glove, slick with my arousal. Struggling anew, I wriggle like a fish on a hook in Tristan's grasp, but he only laughs mockingly and clamps down harder, mask leering at me as he speaks from beneath it.

"Oh, this is going to be fun. Our very own little fuck-doll."

Jameson chuckles, hands back on my leggings. Without any more preamble, he gives a sharp yank, tugging them down to my ankles where they catch around my short boots. Crying, my struggles increase ten-fold. All the helplessness I felt that night flies through my veins at an alarming rate, and the threat of passing out hits me full-force. The sound of a zipper descending is like a gunshot through the quiet of the night, and before I can wriggle even an inch away, Jameson takes my hips in his huge hands and yanks me backward toward himself while Tristan forces me to bend at eye level with his crotch.

Gloved fingers splay my pussy wide, and Jameson groans as my tears gather and spill down my cheeks. There's embarrassment. Shame. A level of futility I had not been expecting. Every horrific thing that I felt as a little girl rushes to the surface, and as Jameson's thick, pearled and pierced cock nudges at my entrance, the chance of escaping this fate is just as dire as the real situation that night.

Having my face bashed in over me not understanding my homework. Watching him hit my mom, holding a knife to her throat, dragging her bloody body around by her hair as she screamed and my cries still rivaled those noises.

With one sharp thrust, he's buried so deep in me it's painful. I cry out before I choke on a sob, but my lips are met with Tristan's cock. Fisting my hair, he positions my mouth how he wants it, making good on his threat to turn me into his fuck-doll as he shoves past my lips and teeth and works his way down my throat. Sobbing, choking, crying, Jameson pounds into me from behind while Tristan fucks me from the front.

Pain swirls with fear and abhorrent memories, and that helplessness grows to the point of explosion as Jameson's deep, steady strokes stretch me wide. Drool cascades down my chin and out of the corners of my mouth. My arms ache, twisted and tied behind me at an odd angle, and the two faceless men begin to morph. The acute pain and humiliation takes on an entirely new form; pleasure blooms from every twinge his pearled cock brings. Tristan swells in my mouth, and instead of gagging and attempting to shake my head loose from his unforgiving grasp, I suck him harder, craving how he stretches my throat. Craving how both of them take my weakness and mold it into vicious power in their strong hands. I am able to bring two of the most powerful men to their knees with a simple look. They are *mine*, and I own their fucking hearts.

Tristan pulls out with a growl, slapping my cheek hard enough to bring a slight sting.

"Such a naughty fucking girl. You like this, huh? Slut," he growls, leaning down until those dead mask eyes stare right into my fucking soul. My mouth drops open as Jameson's pace becomes punishing, my eyes rolling back as a tightness begins to coil in my belly. Tristan's hand flicks up, gripping my cheeks so hard I whimper.

"I bet you'd like two cocks at once, wouldn't you, pretty little butterfly."

An entirely new thrill of fear courses through me, and before I can deny him or plead, Jameson hauls me up until my feet are dangling off the ground and I'm impaled on his cock, his piercing hitting something so deep inside me that it makes sparks of lightning course through every nerve ending. I choke on a sob, for as painful and brutal as it is, it is just as pleasurable, knowing who the men behind the masks are.

Tristan steps forward and Jameson slows his pace, my hands crunched painfully between us. It only serves to make the pleasure that much sweeter. Tristan's tattooed hands lash out, gripping me beneath my thighs, fingers digging in to a painful degree as he lifts my legs and rubs his slippery cock between my pussy lips, hitting my clit with each slow thrust.

"Mmm," I cry, eyes slipping closed.

"You ready to take both of us like such a good girl? You're already doing so well," Jameson growls behind me. Whimpering, my nod is fervent. I need more. I need them to rewire my brain until all I know is pleasure and safety.

And then, I feel him. The heavy tip of Tristan's cock slowly begins to push into my already filled-to-the-brim pussy. My head thuds back onto Jameson's shoulder with a whimper, and I can't help but to curl my face into his neck, breathing his sharp scent in like a drug. Scent will stay with me far longer than anything else, and right now I can feel my brain relaxing, knowing it's him that's so deep inside me, knowing I'll be as close as intimately possible to them both soon enough.

It's a delicate dance, a lot of gentle, shallow thrusting, a back and forth, and Tristan easing his way with his fingers as well. Tristan rips off his mask, wad of spit flying from his mouth to land between our legs. He smears it over my clit, rubbing in slow, languid circles as he feeds me more of himself and Jameson hisses behind me.

"Fuck. God, she's so tight. You're making us so proud, *babochka*," he says, pressing kisses to my temple. I don't remember when he ditched his mask.

"Motherfucker," Tristan growls, face thrown to the black night sky in ecstasy as he feeds me a few more inches. I can't control my moans and whimpers, and each time I do, I receive praise, lingering kisses, hands soothing and warming my body. *I know baby, you're okay, you're doing so well. Fuck, princess, you're so beautiful when you cry. God, you take us so well.*

Jameson stills his thrusting for a moment, and the stretch is an entirely new feeling; there is pain, but there is also such a pleasure from being so fucking filled. Before I can give it much more thought, Tristan's hips meet mine, and their cocks are both squeezed as deeply as they can be inside me.

Jameson is raggedly breathing behind me, and I can hear the grind of Tristan's molars, feel his hot breath fanning over my neck.

"Look down, Alice, look how well you're taking both our cocks deep in your little pussy."

Mewling at what Jameson's words do to me, I obey, Tristan backing away to allow my eyes to feast on such a sight. It's simultaneously frightening as it is arousing. My juices coat their thick, veined shafts, and slow, Jameson begins to pull out.

"Fuck, go slow, I'm gonna come," Tristan grits out.

"Not until she does, *mudak*."

The pearls lining Jameson's shaft drag and pull along my insides, strumming repeatedly against that hidden spot he always knows how to find. As he's almost all the way out, he gently pushes back in, and Tristan begins to pull out.

"Oh…oh my God…" I choke. I'm immediately brought to the edge of an orgasm with one thrust a piece. "Holy fuck."

"We're not your gods, baby," Tristan growls, dragging his thumb over my clit and eliciting a sharp cry from me.

"We're your monsters, your demons, your fucking slaves—and you're the queen of our black hearts."

Tristan begins to push back in as Jameson pulls back out, their rhythm building in pace. I'm nothing but a blubbering mess, filled so deeply that my heart clenches and wrings tears from my eyes again.

"From now until forever," Jameson hisses. "You'll always have our hearts, our little *babochka*."

Their thrusts increase another notch, and I've been coasting on the threat of an immense orgasm for so long now that my knees and legs are shaking. I lost my boots and leggings. I can't make sense of time or space. All I can do is feel such an intense, never-ending pleasure that I know nothing in this world will ever make me feel as high. Clenching my teeth, I try to keep the building scream from escaping as my heart bursts open and my cunt begins to tighten.

"Let us hear you, baby. Let us hear how loudly you love us."

And I do.

I come undone forever, again and again and again as they pound through it, hissing their praises as they try to ride it out, wringing me for every last drop as I squirt streams upon streams on their cocks. And then, I'm filled with their cum, so much that it leaks out of me and runs between my thighs and ass, but they still thrust into me, rutting like wild animals. Another orgasm slices through me at the sight and feeling alone; I'm as full of them as I feel I'll ever be, until I remember:

From now until forever.

I'm theirs forever.

FOLIE À DEUX

EPILOGUE

JAMESON

We spend our time coming down from the high, holding Alice tight between us, sheltering her from the chilly air. She presses her cold, dainty nose to my neck and inhales, sitting in my lap, wrapped in a blanket we brought with us.

"I love how you both smell."

A small smile graces my lips, and my eyes flick to Tristan. He's crouched down, wrapping up Alice's dirty clothes to put in the bag full of necessities we brought. It had been his idea, doing this; Alice had given him head one night and subsequently passed out, leaving her diary wide open. Instead of finding his favorite smut written by our little *babochka's* hand, he'd found her writing about the night her father almost took her and her mother's life, how the experience has never left her.

I hate admitting his next step had been brilliant. He'd been staring at her bookshelf at all the psychology shit she's been devouring for college. He'd found something on rewiring trauma in the brain and presented the idea to me. It hadn't taken long to concoct this plan. And as Tristan's eyes trace lovingly over Alice, I know he feels like he's accomplished something worthy for once. I know, because I feel it, too.

"Are you hurt, baby? You took us so well," I say into her hair. Her shivers stopped a while ago, and she seems more restless and eager to get up and back to her friends. I told her not to worry; we slipped a tracker in Josie's jacket. They're still hopelessly lost in this maze.

Stretching out, she shakes her head, nestling deeper into my embrace. Fuck, the feeling of her in my arms will never cease to take my breath away. She's perfect in her flaws, strong in her sorrow, and brave in her fear. We've given all we have to each other; I know she understands us on a deeper level now. It gives me hope that this will continue to work no matter what life throws our way.

After a little more rest, we walk hand in hand through the maze. Before we get close to the exit, Tristan presses a deep, lingering kiss to Alice's lips, their tongues dancing. Pulling away with a rueful grin at her blushing cheeks, he winks and disappears into the corn.

Turning to her, I run my palms up her puffy jacket sleeves.

"Go straight. We'll watch you from our car to make sure you all get in safe, *da*?"

She nods, her blue eyes bright. Smirking, I swipe my

thumb over her jaw before I lean in and give her a kiss as well. "Such a good girl," I say against her lips.

"Thank you…" she says, trailing off. My teeth bite at her nose as I attempt to hide my grin.

"No thanking us, *babochka*. You're ours, and we protect and cherish what's ours."

She leans up, wrapping her arms around me. I hug her back just as fiercely, pressing a kiss to her warm head before I shoo her away with a sharp slap on her butt. Giggling, she dashes to the exit, almost tempting me to chase her and rut her again in front of everyone. Shaking my head, I turn my sights back to the maze to make sure Ellie is alright; we've had some missed calls from Fordson, and I have a feeling as to why.

Before I get too far, a group comes up the path. Slinking off into the shelter of the dried corn, I slip my mask back on and wait. There's three boys with Seattle Prep sweatshirts, and behind them trail Josie and Ellie. Thank fuck. If we somehow lost the girl Nick Fordson has his eyes on, we wouldn't fucking have eyes.

It's one of his favorite ways to torture his enemies. Man has a thing for ravens and irony.

As soon as they pass, I take the long way around, through the maze to a service road, then behind the concession stands and warming tents. The parking lot is a ways off, but I stop and peel my mask off and hide my knife better. My phone buzzes, and I answer on the second ring as Tristan's name flashes.

"*Da*?" I ask, fixing my boot.

"Get to the car right the fuck now."

I hang up, muscles locking as I take off toward the parking lot. A small crowd has gathered around the two shouting men, one clearly my twin, the other a pale blond with a denim and sheepskin jacket. We parked right next to

Ellie's car, and the evidence is clear; the fucker must have seen Alice and her friends and waited to ambush them when he knew we wouldn't be around.

Shoving my way through the crowd of teens, Alice is the first one I see; face pale as a ghost, eyes wide and glossed with tears. Tristan stands half in front of her, shielding not only her but also Josie and Ellie. The boys from school stand there gawking like idiots.

"Why's he here?" I growl at Tristan in Russian.

He spits at her father's feet before he answers, "Said he had a birthday present for her."

Turning my attention to the piece of shit, I gather all my strength and put it into controlling the urge to rip his arms from his body.

"You need to leave, or we'll involve the police." *Lie.* The police answer to us.

The man has the audacity to chuckle, slipping his hands around his hips, igniting the urge to reach for my gun. The flash of his knife almost has me cackling; I'd tear him to shreds with my teeth before he could get one slice in.

"Get the girls in our car," I seethe to Tristan in our shared language, my eyes never leaving the pale blue of this fucker's. He smirks, but as soon as Tristan starts to pile them into the car, his jaw ticks, his eyes flashing to the rear windows. He wants her as a predator does; wants to take and take until there's nothing left. Wants to make her hurt— make her pay for his stint in prison. I can see it in his eyes.

As if bashing a child's teeth in wasn't enough.

Tristan starts forward, and my hand snaps up, palm slapping across his chest. Through his thick jacket and hoodie, I can feel the angry thumping of his heart. It matches my own.

"You think you two punks scare me?"

Tristan *laughs*, throwing his face to the sky. My

144

answering grin feels as vile and malicious as my plans for this man's death. In those pale eyes flickers the only other drug that even comes close to Alice; his fear.

There's nothing quite like breaking a grown man under your stare, knowing that you're still at the top of the food chain, assured that the predator in you is more ferocious than any beast that stalks this earth. And knowing Alice is just a few feet away, separated by hunks of metal and glass—it makes my inner demons dance. We aren't the two highest paid assassins in the world for no reason.

"No, *podonok*. We *know* we scare you," Tristan says through clenched teeth as though he's a growling Rottweiler. Her father's eyes narrow onto Tristan's chest, onto my hand. I had the sense to remove my leather gloves; they were covered in all manner of heavenly fluids from Alice's perfect cunt. No need to have this piece of shit ruining the best night of our existences.

But as his eyes widen and slowly creep back to my face, the fear from before has completely morphed into abject horror. He takes a trembling step back over the gravelly lot, raising his arms slightly in an attempt to keep something between us. My smile widens, and before my hand slips from Tristan's chest, I can feel his excited tremors, like a police dog quivering in preparation to attack.

I bring my hands in front of me, placing my knuckles into my other palm, splaying my fingers to show off my tattoos in a much clearer way. His throat works up and down as he swallows, eyes flicking from my hand to my face and back in quick succession. The snarling wolf's head on the back of my hand wouldn't alert just anyone to who we are; Tristan has the same one, and the meaning runs deep in the Underworld, an inner network of every government in the world—a black market where any desires can be bought for a stiff price.

One of the most common desires? Murder for hire. Politicians, celebrities, monarchs, even jealous wives. And one thing circles above that sick, twisted world like vultures; *the wolves*. Four families that hold more power than all other powers combined. The Fordsons, the Volkovs, Us—the Stefanovs—and the De Lucas. There's one thing we all bear in common to separate us from the weak, leech-like families; the agreement laid down by our great-grandfathers. It means where one of us ends, another begins, and it means there is nothing we are unwilling to do.

Tristan likes to keep his victims alive until the pain causes a heart attack. I like to bleed them. Nick likes to watch them suffer in the elements for months if it pleases him. Dante likes fire. And fucking Maks…a true psychopath. My birthday gift one year was the head of the man who'd fucked my girl.

And still, as I stare at the man about to piss his pants, I know there's nothing I wouldn't do for Alice, no matter how fucking depraved.

"You know us now, *da?*" I say coolly. He's quick to take another step back with a curt nod. My grin turns to a mordacious snarl. "Then know we'll come for you when it pleases us. I'll have to fight my brother, but in the end, we'll both get what we want."

Throwing his last bit of fear back at us, he growls, "I know people!"

Shaking my head, I catch Tristan's gray eyes. In those depths swirl a love that overshadows his need for destruction; we both found our vulnerability tonight in Alice, but we also found a new kind of strength that I think has surprised us. After a moment, I narrow my eyes and smile.

"I think we have another…*problem.*"

"Shall I?" he asks. My eyes flick to her father as he stumbles back another pace.

"Let's get our *babochka* home for her birthday party. After all, she's been…such a *good girl* lately."

My eyes dare him to say something, and as his jaw ticks, I know he knows, but he's too much of a fucking coward to do anything. Wiping his hand along his face, he walks backward, itching to say something that will make Tristan snap his fucking neck. As soon as he's gone, I open the driver's side door, where I could feel Alice watching me the entire time. I'm met with her big blue eyes, so wide and full of a new kind of awe and wonder. Cheeks pink as a peony in the spring, lips so wet and inviting, her face alone stitches my heart back up, sews me together and keeps me whole and driving forward with purpose. I know she does the same for Tristan.

Reaching up, I cup her face as Josie and Ellie exit. She leans into my palm, her eyes fluttering closed as her small hand grasps mine.

"*Ya tebya lyublyu,*" I whisper against her lips.

Her smile is as dazzling as the sun.

"I love you, too."

BONUS CONTENT

FOLIE À DEUX

BONUS SCENE

ALICE
THE NIGHT BEFORE GRADUATION...

Rain patters the darkened skylight above us, steam swirling upward in silky tendrils and obscuring the view of the tips of black pine trees. With a soft, content smile, I sink further into the scalding water and reminisce on what an amazing year this has turned out to be. Rather unexpectedly, but I'll take whatever small or large victories I can get my hands on. With my graduation from high school just hours away now, the freedom I never thought was tangible is brushing against my fingertips, potent on my tongue.

There's only one thing missing from my current scenario, soaking in Jameson's massive jetted tub, and that's Tristan. I know he's working, and also understand I don't need to know much more than that. But the worry still gnaws on the edges of my frayed nerves. What if something goes wrong? What if he gets hurt? What if—

"*Babochka*," Jameson's sultry, deep voice commands. My eyes spring open, meeting his through the dim, flickering light offered up by numerous candles littering the surface of the counter. The stern look he's giving me churns my stomach in admonishment. Tattooed arms spread across the back of his side of the tub, his chest glistens like some ancient god, his steely jaw set, his lips in a firm line. After a moment, one side of those perfectly sculpted lips quirks up. "Relax. He is fine."

Smiling gently, I nod, but chew the inside of my cheek nonetheless. Whenever one or both of my twins happens to be absent, that festering anxiety builds in my chest. I've lost everyone I love before. I don't think I'd make it if I somehow lost them as well. Before I'm swallowed again by my rampant thoughts, a door downstairs slams shut, and my heart pounds against my ribs in relief and a flood of excitement.

I know without needing to ask of it what will happen when Tristan finds us like this, and as my eyes catch Jameson's, the pit of my stomach tumbles. The hungry, wolfish look in those silvery orbs has my muscles tensing, my cunt clenching. With all the preparations for graduation, we haven't spent much time together lately. I've missed them.

The thunderous stomping of his footfalls alerts us both to his presence, and I turn just in time, the subtle splash of water against the sides of the tub drowning out the sound of my heavily beating heart for a moment. He stands silhouetted in the doorway, broad shoulders filling the width, dark clothes dripping wet, creating a puddle on the black tile at his feet. Even through the darkness, I can see his smirk.

"Started without me I see," he growls, his words aimed at his twin, and a nervously excited smile tugs up the corners of my mouth.

"Barely," I placate quietly, my excitement mingled with trepidation making my throat dry. Trusting them in my core, I'm not afraid they'd ever hurt me; my fears stem from the unknown, the unexplored. There's still so much I know we haven't done, and every encounter brings with it something new, something that pushes me further over the edge of sanity and into madness.

He takes a threatening step toward us, unzipping his sturdy jacket and shrugging out of it. Jameson leans forward, long fingers wrapping around my hips beneath the steaming water as he turns me around and nestles me between his thighs, his cock hard and throbbing against my back, those pearls already rubbing deliciously against my heated, sensitive skin. Lips at my ear, he demands, "You come until you cry and beg for us to stop tonight, *da*? Until you're nothing but a little doll for me to keep fucking."

A shiver runs through me as I gulp, giddiness coursing through me despite the warning of his words. Tristan chuckles, peeling away his short sleeve shirt that clings desperately to his steely torso. His zipper descends next, revealing the fact that he's forgone any boxers. Tugging down his jeans, he kicks them aside and stands proudly before us, stroking his rigid length.

"Did you give her our surprise, brother?" he asks huskily. Jameson's throaty chuckle against the back of my neck as he trails his nose up to the base of my skull has me shivering anew, eyes slitted in cresting ecstasy.

153

FOLIE À DEUX

"Which one?"

Tristan steps rather gracefully into the tub, sinking down, knees to chest as he adjusts to fit his frame in the tub. My eyes catch his rueful smirk.

"The one you do not like."

Jameson growls against me possessively now, dragging his wet fingers up my shoulder to the hair at the nape of my neck, sinking them into the tendrils and giving a sharp tug backwards. With a light gasp, I obey his silent demand, my nails digging into his thighs.

"Her skin is too beautiful to be ruined with ink."

He gives a shallow cant of his hips against me, his cock strumming along my spine, and I'm barely able to decipher what his words mean. When it clicks into place, I ask with giddiness, "A tattoo?"

Tristan grins and dips his chin once. "*Da*, little girl. Whatever you want, as long as—"

"A butterfly," I rasp, Jameson's lips suckling at that one spot behind my ear that makes me moan. Both of them chuckle now, and Tristan reaches forward, hands traveling up my sides before cupping my breasts, pinching and rolling my stiff nipples between thumb and forefinger. A whine of need escapes me.

"Why?" he teases. "Because we've trapped you like a pretty little butterfly?"

Jameson's hand slips down my belly, heading toward the crest at the juncture of my thighs that aches and throbs for his expert touch. I can barely nod, but I manage.

"She's missed this," Jameson says, the pads of his fingers finally finding my clit. My body lurches at his electric touch, hips bucking upward as I silently beg for more. Tristan's fingers leave my nipples, diving down beneath the water to find my entrance already slick, eager.

"Let me feel how much you missed me," he demands,

sinking two fingers into my pussy.

"Fuck," I moan, sated, complete in some sense but needing more. I begin to grind my hips against his still fingers, fucking myself on him.

"Always such a needy little whore," Jameson growls, hand leaving my hair, the crack of his skin against my breast like a strike of lightning. The sting that follows is soothed only by the subtle shifting of Tristan's fingers as he languidly pumps them into me now.

"I think our little cum slut is ready for more," Tristan says, and I nod without a thought in my mind.

"Careful what you wish for," Jameson warns. "Tristan has been waiting for this."

A thrill of fear courses through my veins, heightening the pleasure building in my cunt with each stroke of his fingers. Jameson lifts me, placing me on his lap, spreading my thighs as wide as the tub allows and tilting my hips upward as he winds his arms beneath my knees. While keeping his fingers planted in me, Tristan reaches for something, and my eyes widen in the darkness as he brandishes a toy I've never seen before, but something I seem to understand the purpose of rather quickly.

It's clear, like an icicle, with nodules that grow in circumference until they reach an impossibly large ball at the base.

"I can't wait to fuck your cunt with your ass filled and vibrating," he says, coating the toy in lube. Lips trembling, I whine as he removes his fingers and instead positions the toy at the entrance of my ass. I've taken their fingers, and their cocks, but nothing like this before.

He leans forward, brushing his lips against mine.

"Take it like a good slut," Jameson whispers in my ear. Eyes rounded in trepidation, Tristan sinks his two middle fingers back into my cunt and forces the first nodule past the tight band of resistance at my ass. Heart pounding, the moan that escapes me is throaty and fills the echoing bathroom. Already, I feel so full, but I want more—*need* more.

"More, please," I beg as he makes a 'come here' motion with his fingers inside me. Jameson begins to play with my nipples, pinching and twisting them, bending me to his will as I become a puddle of nothingness between them.

"So polite," Tristan says. "You'll be begging for the opposite when I'm balls deep in this cunt, and I won't be able to oblige, then."

My eyes roll back at his words, and with a twist and thrust, he pops the next two nodules into my ass, shallowly thrusting his fingers at the same time. Jameson pinches my clit between his knuckles, and I cry out, a deep, entirely new type of climax budding between my thighs.

Tristan works the toy into me little by little, and Jameson soothes the different type of ache as he slowly circles my clit. Before long, I'm a shaking, crying mess.

"I...I can't...take any...anymore," I breathe, thighs quivering. The entire toy is nearly inside me, but Tristan doesn't stop, slowly yet forcefully fitting the last ball into me. "Ahh!" I cry, gritting my teeth. He wrenches his fingers out of me, and without warning, the toy turns on, a low, pulsating vibration coursing through my ass and deep in my pussy at the same time.

Placing his palms on my knees, he forces me somehow further apart and lines the head of his cock to the tight entrance of my pussy.

"You're so pretty Alice," Jameson says. "Take his cock like such a good little slut."

And I have no choice but to obey as he sinks his length and girth into me in one ruthless thrust. I'm so full it feels impossible. He sets a pace that has me panting and moaning and crying out to the night, water sloshing over the side of the tub like little tsunamis.

"Come hard for me, let me fill you up, baby," Tristan pants, fucking me hard and fast, hand finding my throat, fingers sinking into my mouth. I whine against him, my own tidal wave building. Attempting to hold out, to cling to the pleasure for as long as I can, I ride the wave of ecstasy, my breath halting in my lungs, time and space suspended as the pumping of his cock and the vibrations of the toy course through me. Stomach tightening into a knot, it unravels like a spool of yarn, and I scream against his fingers, withering around him, my pussy clenching his girth over and over.

"Yes," he hisses, hips stuttering as he spills his sticky cum into me. Breathing heavily, he pulls out all too quickly, but the absence of his warmth and girth is quickly replaced by Jameson's, his pearls and piercings ramming hard into me.

"Higher," he grits out, and the vibrations in my ass double as I shake still from my first orgasm.

"Oh…oh my God," I cry, trembling as he pumps into me furiously from behind.

"More," he demands.

"What…no!" I cry, but Tristan just chuckles breathlessly, obeying his twin, and the vibrations are now impossibly strong, Jameson's pearled cock rubbing against the toy in my ass with nothing but a thin band of muscle separating us.

My eyes widen, however, when I see that Tristan is hard again, his gaze stuck on my filled ass and pussy.

"Make room for me," he hisses, and Jameson's rhythm stutters briefly before stopping.

"No…no, I can't!" I plead, pushing against Tristan's slick chest. My strength is feeble and nothing compared to theirs, and he simply laughs in my face, lining up his cock to my pussy again, thrusting in as Jameson pulls out. Tears spring into my eyes, and Jameson clamps a hand over my mouth, cutting off my pleas and cries as they work themselves into my sore cunt.

"Fuck," Tristan groans. "So fucking tight for us."

Soon, they're thrusting in tandem, and it feels as though I am being split in two, my head lolling from side to side on Jameson's shoulder, my eyes rolling back, his hand still keeping my cries locked away as tears stream down my cheeks, another orgasm looming for all of us. The moment Tristan pinches my clit and rubs his thumb over it, I scream against Jameson's palm and come undone, the clenching of my pussy so harsh it nearly forces them out of me. But they both bear down, fucking me through it, filling me until I overflow with their cum.

And as we all pant and soak in the bliss we've created from the ashes of our lives, I know in my soul there is nothing I wouldn't do for the men I endlessly love.

CONTACT

Did you love this story? Don't be shy! Leave a review on Amazon, Goodreads, or any other platform. Want to know more about the author or strike up a chat? Follow: rubymedjoromance on Instagram for daily updates on new works, or shoot her an email at: rubymedjoromance@ gmail.com

SNEAK PEEK:

Want an exclusive sneak peek of *The Game (Book One in the Villainous Heroes Series)*? Out now!

FOLIE À DEUX

ALICE WINTERS
JUNE, 2022

Their beaming faces will always stand out from the imposing crowd. My eyes stay locked on theirs the entire time I am on that stage. Through Ellie's valedictorian speech, through our principal's droning on and on about what bright futures we have ahead of us. The sun streams down in golden rays, and the polyester black gown I wear traps the heat and makes sweat trickle down my spine. But none of that matters.

The moment my name is called, I stand on shaky legs, nervous as can be. If I trip and face plant, that will be the last memory this school has of me. So with my head held high, and a grin stretching my cheeks to a painful degree, my heels scrape across the rickety stage, and my sweaty hand clasps the school board president's as he holds out my diploma. Squaring my shoulders to the crowd to allow for a photo op as I've been instructed, my eyes again find them; my twins, the men I love.

Jameson's phone is turned sideways as he films, but behind the black rectangle, I can see his very own rare grin, one that gives him laugh lines only Tristan and I can bring out.

And then there's Tristan, beaming proudly, a mischievous glint in his steely eyes as he raises a red horn and fires off the noise, the elderly couple next to them shooting them vehement glares. The laugh that bubbles up my chest is unhindered by my past, by the tragedy that struck my life not long ago. I wish my mother and step-father were here to see this day, to see that their efforts in raising me paid off. I've been accepted to the University of Washington for the psychology program, and with Ellie's help writing my essays, I have enough in scholarships to pay for half of my tuition each year for four years.

Tristan and Jameson eagerly shoved money at me for schooling, but this was something I'd always intended to do on my own. I want something that is solely mine, something I will work for, something that will pave the way for me to help others in need.

The board member drops my hand as the next name is called, and I carefully pick my way over cords and around microphone stands until I am back to the risers behind the podium. Josie is next to me, holding out her fist. Bumping mine with hers, my heart flutters anew. This is really it. I've graduated high school. The world is at my feet. We can move, we can have our relationship become public as soon as we're away from prying eyes and old money. Of all the bad I've endured in my life, it brought me to this point in time, and I cannot help but to be thankful for it.

Until my eyes sweep across the back of the crowd and land upon my father's.

THANK YOU:

Phew! Another one bites the dust! Tackling a novella that turned into a prequel was an entirely new challenge for me, but I always love pushing my own boundaries. I don't think I've ever had to research for a book as much as I did for this one, but I wanted to ensure I was creating something deeply forbidden and taboo yet still *right*, if that makes sense. All in all, it was so fun to create these characters and throw all my cautions to the wind and let all their dirty desires speak for themselves!

Here are my major thank yous!

To Jenn, my beta reader. Thank you for taking a gamble on me, making me laugh so freaking hard, and for gracing us all with your book recs, reels, and hilarious Tik Toks.

To my ARC team: what a way to kick off 2022! Y'all make me smile and keep pushing me to always do better and to keep creating even when I'm grumpy and don't want to. You've all supported me more than you know and I cannot wait to keep sharing all the goodies in my mind with you!

To Charly: this cover redesign and formatting…it makes me cry tears of joy. I love seeing how Alice is reflected, and all of the little hints and nods to the story within. It is simply perfect, and I cannot thank you enough for doing such a stellar job.

And to my love: we've had to rewrite the stars a few times, but the love we have for each other only seems to grow stronger with every obstacle we face. You are my safe place, my person. Love to me is a choice as much as it is a feeling, and I am so grateful that we choose each other day after day. The best for us is yet to come.

ABOUT THE AUTHOR

Ruby Medjo is a graduate of the English program at Eastern Washington University, where she cultivated and refined her passion for telling stories. Currently residing in the gorgeous Pacific Northwest, she spends her time reading, writing, drinking coffee (or wine), and teaching her English and History classes. She is blessed to be surrounded by amazing friends and family who continue to push her to pursue her dreams no matter how intimidating. She is still waiting on her Hogwarts acceptance letter, but she is now willing to fall through the stones at Craigh na Dune instead.

www.ingramcontent.com/pod-product-compliance
Lightning Source LLC
Chambersburg PA
CBHW071515170626
46811CB00007B/2863